SINFUL
INTENT

ALFA INVESTIGATIONS

Publisher © Chelle Bliss July 14th 2015
Edited by Silently Correcting Your Grammar
Proofreader Deaton Author Services
Cover Design © Lori Jackson Designs
Formatted by Allusion Graphics, LLC

SINFUL
INTENT

ALFA INVESTIGATIONS

CHELLE BLISS

"A perfect mix of suspense, steam, and love. Bliss never fails to hook me from page one and have me wishing the book wouldn't end. Another must-click!" ~ *Harper Sloan, NYT Bestselling author of the Corps Security Series*

"The ALFA PI series in an exciting new rush, like being on a brand new roller coaster, and I can't wait to experience the whole ride!" ~ *Christine R. - Nice Ladies, Naughty Books*

"I could not put it down and cannot wait for the next book. It is a phenomenal read and Chelle gets better and better with every book!" ~ *Cat Mason, Author of the Shaft on Tour Series*

"Sinful Intent, by the amazing Chelle Bliss, is a raw, riveting, rewarding, and romantic roller coaster of a read that will swallow your heart and soul, and scorch your panties." ~ *Karen M - Bookalicious Babes Blog*

"I didn't think I could possibly like this new series as much as I liked Men of Inked... Chelle has worked her magic and proved me wrong." ~ *Michelle E. - Literature Litehouse*

"God do I love it when Chelle Bliss puts the pen to paper, or the fingers to the keyboard. She creates an epic tale each and every time!" ~ *Shelly L. – Sexy Book Reviews*

"It's an interactive experience that will cause you to smile, frown, laugh, gasp, giggle, and blush." ~ *Rosarita Reader*

"This is my first book by Chelle Bliss and it won't be my last." ~ *CP Smith, Author of the Reason Series*

"What a roller coaster ride!!" ~ *Shay L. – Mommy's a Book Whore*

"Chelle Bliss starts her ALFA series off with bang! Sinful Intent is deliciously sexy and absolutely thrilling from beginning to end. This book is sure to be your next best read." ~ *Nita Bee - The Book Chick*

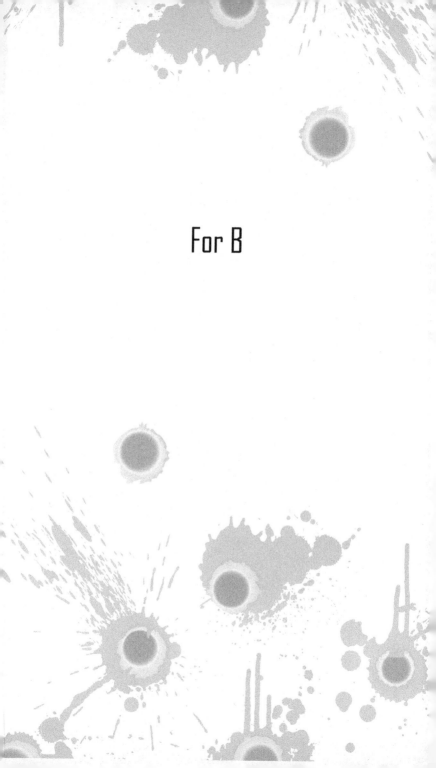

For B

PROLOGUE

"All right, Ma." I dig through the pile of unopened mail to find the invitation I'd ignored.

"You need to see your family. It'll do you good to be around the Gallo side."

"Why?" I don't know why I asked. I already knew the answer. They were her side and, therefore, superior.

My Ma, Fran DeLuca, had been on my back since the day I'd come home from the army. I loved the hell out of the woman, but she could be a major pain in my ass.

"They have their lives together. Sal knew how to raise boys."

My jaw tightened. "Are you saying I'm not a good man, Ma?"

"Morgan, you know that's not what I meant. You need to get out of this city for a little while and clear your head. Plus," she added, drawing out the S, "I need you to accompany me on the trip. You know I hate traveling alone. The suitcase is always too heavy for me to lift, and I get lost easily."

I closed my eyes and exhaled. "Fine, Ma. I'll take you to Izzy's wedding. But I won't be happy about it."

"Thank you, baby. I'll call now and tell your aunt Maria to expect us. I want to get there a couple of days early. I'll book the airfare. You just show up sober enough to be allowed on the plane, Morgan. Understand?"

She showed up at my place, without calling, after I'd had a few beers while watching football. She immediately jumped to the conclusion that I was a closet drinker and I've never been able to convince her otherwise.

"Ma, I'm not a drunk, for Christ's sake." I pinched the bridge of my nose.

"I love you," she said as she disconnected the call.

Fan-fucking-tastic.

I hadn't seen the Gallos in ages. Izzy had been a gawky teenager with a sharp tongue, and the boys... they were Gallo through and through. They were tough, rough, and always looking for an angle.

I wouldn't say that I was very different from them, but the bloodline had been watered down with the addition of my father's side. They were the better half of the family tree.

At least I could spend a couple of days in the sunshine instead of freezing my balls off in Chicago. My mother would have my full attention and use the time to chew my ear off about why didn't I find a good woman to settle down with already—it was the same conversation we'd had almost every day for the last month.

Before I could even get up from the table, my phone rang again.

"What now, Ma?" I pushed the chair back.

"I spoke to your aunt and everything is set. You're going to stay with Joe while we're there, and I'll stay with Mar and Sal."

"Do I get a choice in this?" I stood, wandering over to the floor-to-ceiling windows that overlooked the city.

"Nope. Everyone else is full. Joey will be happy to have you."

"I'm going to get a hotel."

I hated staying with people, especially when I hadn't seen that person in ten years. I knew them as well as I knew my father, and he walked out of our lives the day I graduated from high school.

"No, you're not. That would be such a slap in the face. You'll stay with Joe and Suzy."

"We'll talk about it later. I have shit to do."

"Start packing, Morgan. I'll book our tickets for the day after tomorrow." *Click.*

Ma was the queen of hanging up before I could say anything more.

Staring out at Lake Michigan, I rolled my neck and counted to ten. I could handle a few days with the family.

Maybe they'd help get my mind off all the fucked-up shit I'd seen. My faith in humanity had evaporated while I'd been in combat, but the silence and calm of being a civilian had me climbing the freaking walls.

I needed to get out of here.

Old friends, the kind who were trouble, had been lighting up my phone since the day I returned. They weren't the type of people I needed to be hanging out with.

As a kid, I found myself in trouble more times than I liked to remember—small crimes, petty theft, and other bullshit things kids do. The last straw came when we stole a car and were quickly popped for the crime.

Instead of spending time in jail, I was given an option—enter the service and turn my life around or head to the slammer and do some time.

The military seemed like the better choice. At least I'd be free and see the world. But the only part of the world I'd seen resembled a barren wasteland, not even close to the tropical paradise the brochures promoted.

I'll say one thing about the military—it did straighten my ass out and made me a man. I wasn't the same punk who'd left for basic training.

The last thing I needed was to hook up with my *buddies* who had never left "the life." I knew they were still pulling jobs that could land them in prison for much of their natural life. I'd finally been given my freedom back, and there was no way in hell I'd give it up to make a quick buck.

Spending quality time with my quiet family should help me unwind and figure out my future, right?

Who was I kidding?

The Gallos had never been quiet a day in their lives. They were loud and obnoxious, but they were my family, and it would be nice to spend time with them.

It was time to get my shit in order, head down to the Florida sunshine, and get the fuck away from the Windy City.

CHAPTER ONE

MORGAN

Opportunities

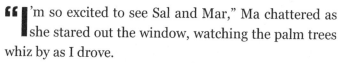

"I'm so excited to see Sal and Mar," Ma chattered as she stared out the window, watching the palm trees whiz by as I drove.

"I hope she has food. I'm starving. What's with the peanuts on a three-hour flight?" I glanced at the GPS.

We were close, within ten minutes of their house.

"Do you think about anything but food?"

"Yep." There was so much on my mind, but in that moment, all I could think of was a home-cooked meal. The thing I remembered the most about Aunt Mar was her food. Ma wasn't a good cook, but we made do. When we'd visit the Gallos, I made sure to memorize every taste until the next trip. "But right now I need to eat."

"I can't wait to wrap my arms around my brother. It's a shame I haven't been back in so long." She fidgeted clicking her fingernails together.

"Why haven't you, Ma? We used to come here all the time, and then you stopped visiting."

She placed her hand on my arm. "I felt ashamed after your father left. I couldn't bring myself to face them."

"Ma, if they judge you—"

5

"No, no, Morgan." She brushed her fingers against my skin. "They aren't like that. It was all in my head. Then you left for the army and I was scared to go anywhere."

I glanced at her. "What do you mean you were scared?"

"I always waited for the man to come tell me that my son died serving his country. I was too petrified to go anywhere in case I'd miss that."

"Jesus." I gripped the steering wheel tighter. "That's the dumbest shit I've ever heard."

Her hand flew from my arm and smacked me upside the head. "You just had to sign up for the army," she nagged as her voice grew nasally. "You couldn't go off to college like the rest of the kids. I had enough stress in my life besides having my only child serve during a time of war."

That was classic Fran DeLuca.

Hard-core nag and guilt-tripper extraordinaire.

I cursed the gods every day for making me an only child. She gave me all of her attention. Sure, it had been great when I was a little kid, but now? Not so much.

When my father left, I knew she'd be up my ass. That's one of the reasons I decided to join the army. I wanted to get away from everything, including her attention. I couldn't imagine if I ended up in jail—she'd probably visit every day to yell at me.

"Can you be any more dramatic?" I shifted my eyes, glancing at her.

"I saw the names of the soldiers killed in action as I watched the news each night. Do you know what that does to a mother?" Her voice was almost shrill.

"I'm sure you're gonna tell me."

"You're lucky I love you." She stared out the window again.

"Uh-huh," I replied as I pulled onto the freeway exit, getting one step closer to the Gallos.

This entire week, my mother would be out of my hair. She'd be too wrapped up in her brother and sister-in-law to care about what I did.

The rest of the way, we drove in silence.

"You have arrived," the robotic GPS voice stated.

"I remember it being bigger." I took in the sight of their house.

"It's the same, but you were small."

"I was never small." I put the car in park.

"You're so full of shit, Morgan. Let's go. I can't sit here another minute." She opened the door and climbed out quicker than I'd seen her move in years.

Turning off the car, I started to pray as I climbed out. "God grant me the serenity."

"Franny!" Aunt Mar came running out the front door with her arms outstretched. Uncle Sal strolled behind her like his usual cool self, looking like it was just another day and he was heading to the grocery store.

"Mar!" Ma yelled back, jogging toward her.

It was going to be one of those weeks. Loud, loving, and sweet enough to make my teeth hurt. I leaned against the car with my arms crossed and watched the scene unfold.

I couldn't remember the last time I'd seen my mother as happy as she looked in that moment.

One by one, my cousins piled out of the house, but a few new faces followed them.

"Yo!" Mike stalked down the driveway toward me.

7

The boy had grown into a man. He was beyond jarhead size; the man was built like a brick shithouse. Then I spotted a drop-dead gorgeous brunette standing next to him.

"Hey, shithead," I replied as he got closer. "Lookin' bigger than ever."

"Fuck off, dickface. Gimme a hug, big man." He held out his arms to me.

I rolled my eyes as he put his arms around me. "You people are way too touchy-feely for me," I muttered as he smashed my body.

Mr. Ray DeLuca hadn't been a hugger. My mother showered love on me, but rarely did I ever experience it from another man. Only when we visited Ma's side of the family did I realize I'd missed out.

"You're such a whiny bitch, Morgan."

"I've heard you've turned into quite the pussy." I jabbed him in the ribs.

"Was that a fly or did you hit me?" He backed away, holding my shoulders and laughed. "It's so good to see you, li'l cousin."

"You too, Mikey."

He slapped me on the shoulder, almost throwing me off-kilter. "You're still an asshole. That's why you're my favorite cousin," he said with a grin.

Peering over his shoulder, I gawked at his woman. She had pink cheeks, wild curls that fell over her shoulders, and matching warm brown eyes that sparkled in the sunlight. "Who do we have here?" I asked, giving her my best smile.

Mike cleared his throat; his glare was inescapable as he wrapped his arm tightly around her waist. "This is my wife, Mia." He emphasized the wife part.

"It's a pleasure meeting you, Mia." I reached for her hand.

"She's mine," Mike warned, pulling Mia toward him.

She gave me a playful smirk. "Hey, handsome."

Mike pulled her closer. "Mia," he snarled.

"Get over yourself, Michael. It's your cousin," she told him, motioning toward me as she pried herself from his grip.

"Oh, I like her already."

"Hey, little cousin." Thomas pulled me into a bear hug with a beautiful redhead standing behind him. "It's so good to see you, man."

"It's nice to see you made it out alive." His years undercover had aged him, but his getting out in one piece was nothing short of miraculous.

"I could say the same to you. I want you to meet my wife, Angel."

"Hi, Morgan. It's wonderful to meet you." She held her hand out.

Instead of taking her hand, I did it the Gallo way and wrapped her in my arms. "It's wonderful to meet you, Angel," I whispered before releasing her.

"Morgan!" a woman screeched from behind Angel, pushing her out of the way. "I've missed you!"

"Izzy?" I looked down at her and shook my head, shocked that she was no longer the little girl I'd pictured.

My little cousin Izzy had always been beautiful— well, maybe not during that awkward teenage phase. When she was little, she'd follow us around, trying to do whatever we were. I couldn't imagine dealing with a little sister all the time. I would've gone batshit crazy.

"You've grown more beautiful with age," I teased, but it was the truth.

"You're still a bullshitter, DeLuca." She kicked the dirt near her feet much like she had when she was a little girl.

"Where's my hug from the bride-to-be?"

She flung herself into my arms. As I squeezed her, I watched as Ma greeted everybody with a giant smile on her face.

"You're like hugging a damn hard teddy bear." Izzy's fingers dug into my back.

"Must be a Gallo thing," I replied, noticing that I was similar in size to her brothers.

"Choking me," she whined with a strangled voice.

"Sorry, babe." I set her feet on the ground.

"You're a big lug." She laughed as Auntie Mar approached us.

There was something weird about seeing my family after having been apart for many years. Although they were different people and had grown older, we fell in like old times. The familiarity hadn't vanished. We shared memories of the way things used to be, and that drew us together, making us one.

The number of new names I'd have to remember was daunting. Angel was Thomas's wife, James was Izzy's husband-to-be, Max was Anthony's wife, Suzy was Joe's wife, and Mia was Mike's. Plus, they each had children. Maybe by the end of the trip I'd have the names down pat. It was enough to make my head spin.

"Hey, Auntie Mar. I've missed you."

"Hey, kiddo." She smiled, tilting her head up and looking at me. "Morgan, my dear, you just want to eat my food. I haven't forgotten," she said as she rubbed my stomach.

"True, but that doesn't mean I didn't miss you too." I rubbed my stomach where her hand had just been. "But your sauce is something that can't be explained, and based on my Ma's cooking, it can't be replicated either." I waited for Ma to slap me again.

Scanning the yard, I noticed that Ma was too far to hear or reach me even if she had.

"You're lucky she didn't hear you." Aunt Mar wrapped her arms around my waist and rested her head on my chest. "I'm so happy you're home safe. We were so worried about you."

I hugged her back, feeling a bit warm and fuzzy inside. I'd always loved Auntie Mar the most out of any of my relatives. "I made it out alive."

"You're the last thing your Ma has." She peered up at me. "If something were to happen to you, she'd lose it."

I refrained from rolling my eyes. "Thanks for more of a guilt trip, Auntie Mar."

"It's a family thing."

"Yeah, and something I could do without."

"Let's get some food in you and maybe you won't feel so grumpy."

"Couldn't think of anything more perfect." I kissed the top of her head.

We headed up the driveway along with my cousins and their other halves. The crew had quadrupled if I counted the kids.

Suddenly, I felt behind in the family department.

Shit. Was I going to be stuck with Ma as my plus-one for an eternity?

I collapsed on the couch. Why hadn't I worn sweat pants? I had known I'd overeat, but I hadn't wanted to greet my family looking like a slob. Let's be real. If I'd shown up to the airport in sweats, Fran would've had a conniption.

Being in the living room, looking around at my family, I felt genuinely happy. When I was a kid, I used to beg my parents to let me stay with Auntie Mar for the summer just so I could feast on her amazing cooking, but Ma always said no. She claimed that they had enough children to worry about without having to feed me every day.

"So, what are you doing with yourself now?" Joe asked as I yawned.

Joe had always been a tough-lookin' guy. Even as a teenager, he had the look that had others cower around him. His tattoos, his wide torso, and fuck-off look that had become permanently etched on his face made him even more intimidating.

"Trying to digest. Other than that, not a damn thing." I closed my eyes.

"Must you always be a smartass?" Anthony asked.

He was the oldest of the Gallo kids. He'd always been artsy, interested in music at a young age, and had shied away from the bullshit Joe and I had found ourselves in as kids. He was an old soul, but he wasn't the touchy-feely type. The one thing he had a talent for besides music was women. His cup overflowed with pussy, and he made no apologies.

"That's ripe coming from you." I could feel the food coma starting to grip my body.

Anthony had always been the biggest smartass. He'd never been as physically big as his brothers, or as athletic, but he used his words as weapons. His calling me a smartass was the funniest damn thing in the world.

"Have you found a job?" Thomas sat down next to me.

The wear and tear from Thomas's time undercover lined his face. He looked older than the others now, the stress permanently etched on his tanned skin.

"Nothing yet. I haven't even bothered to look, really. I'm just trying to settle back into civilian life."

"It's freaky shit, isn't it? Nothing feels right anymore. Happened to me when I finished working undercover for the DEA. It took me a good year before things felt normal again."

"Yeah," I replied, too tired to say anything more. I stretched, trying to wake myself up. I needed to sit up to stay awake. This was utterly ridiculous.

"What did you do in the army?" Izzy sat down next to her fiancé James.

James was the perfect partner for her. I could tell. I'd always thought I had a knack for reading people. James obviously didn't put up with her bullshit. She needed a man more overbearing than her brothers or she'd eat him alive. James and Thomas had become best friends when they'd worked together in the DEA, and they'd started a business together a year ago.

I leaned forward and took a deep breath. "I was a cavalry scout and did recon work."

"Interesting." James rubbed his chin and stared at me.

"Sometimes it could be. Basically, I was the eyes and ears for the troops on the battlefield."

James turned to Thomas and raised an eyebrow. "You know what I'm thinking?"

"Yep, and we'll talk about it later," Thomas replied as he rubbed his hands together, glancing at me.

They nodded to each other, and James turned his attention back to me. "How long did you serve?"

"Served eight years."

"Thanks for your service," Suzy, Joe's girl, said as she held their daughter, Gigi.

"Any time, beautiful." Out of the corner of my eye I could see Joe staring at me. "It's impressive that each of you found a beautiful woman."

"Looks aren't everything, man," Anthony said.

"Says the man with the exotic beauty in the next room," I teased him. "I'm not being a dick. I'm just making an observation."

"Well, you can keep those thoughts to yourself, buddy," Mike warned, puffing out his chest.

They were so uptight.

"Let me say this. They are your women. I'll never try anything or get in between you. I respect your relationships entirely. I'm just making a statement. You've all done well for yourselves. I'm hoping that, someday, I'm lucky enough to find someone for myself. We're family. I'd never fuck with family."

"Watch your mouth." Ma smacked my head.

My body jolted and I cursed under my breath. I hadn't seen her enter the room behind me. I swear she'd lurk in the shadows just to whack me.

"Yes, Ma." I turned toward Joe. "Thanks for letting me stay with you."

"I'm pretty close to rethinking that now, Morgan." He smirked, running his hand up Suzy's leg.

"Come on, man. I'll be a perfect gentleman." I meant every word of it, too.

I'd never try anything with their ladies. I knew I could be a total jackass, but that was beyond even my level of assholishness.

Suzy set Gigi on the floor and climbed into Joe's lap. "Stop being so serious all the time. He can help with Gigi while you're at work."

I shook my head and waved my hands. "Oh, no. I couldn't. I'm not good with kids anyway." Fuck, I'd never really been around little ones.

"You'll be fine. Gigi likes you."

"No, she doesn't," I replied, staring at Gigi, who couldn't have cared less about me as she played with a Barbie.

"She likes everyone." Suzy smiled at Joe.

"Just like her mother." Joe's eyes shot up toward the ceiling as he mumbled something and rubbed his face.

"Joseph," Suzy warned, "you'll be nice to our guest this week."

"Anything for you, sugar." He gave her a kiss and brought her closer to his body.

"I can get a hotel," I interrupted, feeling like a third wheel.

He tucked his face into her neck. "Nah, man. Stay with us. We have plenty of room. We actually have a guesthouse on the property. You'll have it to yourself."

I whistled, impressed that my cousin had a pad swanky enough to have a guesthouse.

"Suzy's friends used to rent it, but it's been empty since they moved out."

"I may never leave," I teased.

"Dessert!" Auntie Mar yelled from the dining room.

My stomach growled, and I looked down, trying to figure out how I'd fit another bite of food in my body. "How do you guys stay so damn fit with her cooking?"

"It's a challenge, bro." Thomas walked past and slapped me on the shoulder. "Lots of working out and physical activity."

It took me two attempts to push myself off the couch before I was able to stagger to my feet. "I'd have to spend all my free time at the gym if I ate her food every day."

"You won't have that problem with Suzy's cooking," Izzy teased as she followed me into the dining room.

"She lured me by other means," Joe said before he pulled Suzy into his arms and gave her a deep kiss.

Being around the Gallos kind of made my head hurt and my heart ache. They never stopped talking or teasing each other, but the amount of love in the house made me long for something I'd never had.

I grabbed a slice of cake and headed back to the living room, trying to get a moment's peace. Before my ass hit the couch cushion, Mike strolled into the room.

"So," he said before he stuffed a forkful of cake in his mouth. "I know you have some shit going on up there. Fess up." Small crumbs fell from his lips, landing on his lap as he spoke.

"Not a thing, Mike," I replied before scooping the frosting off the cake and shoving it in my mouth.

"Liar. Back in the game?" He cocked an eyebrow.

"Nope."

He stared at me as if he were trying to figure out if I was bullshitting him or not. "Fine. Are you getting back in, then?"

I shook my head. "Nah. I'm too old to do any time in the joint, man. It's not worth it anymore. I was given my one chance at redemption, and I doubt I'd get a second if I got caught."

Mike laughed. "You always were a lucky SOB. I mean, we had to move because of all the shit you started to get Joe involved in. Ma did not want him to be a criminal."

"Oh, please. Joe would've never been a criminal."

"Don't be so sure. He's still scary as fuck. Hey, why don't you move down here, dude? I mean, the weather sucks in Chicago. You don't have a job. You'd have us. What could be bad?"

I savored another bite of cake, wishing I could eat like this every week. "I don't know. I don't think my mother would survive without me."

"She'll be fine."

"Dude, you clearly don't know Fran that well. She's up in my shit all the time." I scraped my fork against the plate, gathering every morsel left before putting it in my mouth. "She'd go bananas if I moved away," I mumbled.

"Have her come too." He shrugged, not meeting my eyes.

"Chicago is a big city. I could get lost and not see her for weeks if I wanted to. Here, it's a little too close for comfort, if ya know what I mean."

"Yeah." He leaned back and polished off the cake.

"What are you talking about in here?" Thomas walked in, rubbing his gut.

"I'm trying to get Morgan to move down here, T," Mike replied, setting his empty plate on the coffee table.

"James and I were just talking about that. We could use another guy on our team. You have the skills we need and you're family," Thomas said as he sat across from me in his father's chair and leaned forward.

"What do you do again?" I asked, forgetting what Ma had told me.

"James and I started a private investigations company a while back. It's become such a success that we have a backlog of cases and often have to turn people away. So what do you say?"

I could easily be a PI. It didn't seem like that hard of a job. The army had given me the skills necessary for the part.

"I'll think about it." I chewed my lip, mulling his words over. "I need a few days to make a decision."

"The offer stands." Thomas reached into his pocket and pulled a business card out. "When you have a decision, call me or stop by the office."

I took the card and read it.

Thomas Gallo
Owner
ALFA Private Investigation

Underneath was the contact information for the office and his cell phone number.

I flipped it in my fingers and nodded. "I'll let you know as soon as I figure shit out. Don't mention a word of it to Fran."

The last thing I wanted was for her to go berserk before the wedding. Thomas and Mike both laughed.

"We got your back," Thomas said.

Suzy and Joe had been gracious hosts. They had made sure I'd wanted for nothing while I'd stayed with them. Most likely out of fear that word would get back to Auntie Mar.

I'd always thought of my big cousin Joe as somewhat of a badass when we were kids. Spending a couple of days with him had me learning about the real man.

He was always kind to his wife, showing the utmost patience and care. He was over the top with his daughter and never became flustered. He was everything I looked up to in a man and nothing I'd grown up having.

I'd gained mad respect for him in the three days I'd spent with them waiting for the wedding. I'd tried to get lost during the day, not wanting to be the new babysitter. Every evening, Joe and I would enjoy a beer and chat before we both headed to bed.

"You know, if you stay," he said as he tossed his beer can in the trash can while we sat on the stone patio of the guesthouse, "you can rent this until you find a place of your own."

"Thanks, Joe. It's kind of you to still want me around." I grinned.

"I learned that you aren't as big of an asshole as you make yourself out to be."

"Joe," I said as I stood, "don't tell anyone that. I like for people to think I'm a giant prick."

"I won't let your secret out as long as you don't tell people about me."

"I know. I figured that out already."

"I gotta hit the sack. Ma will have my head if I'm late to the wedding tomorrow."

I nodded, knowing we'd all have hell to pay if we didn't arrive on time. "Sleep well, cousin."

He walked back toward the main house, giving me time alone. I'd built a small fire in the pit earlier, and I decided to watch it as it burned out.

The night sky in Florida was different than back home. The bright lights of the city drowned out the twinkle of the stars. Here, underneath the country sky, with the nearest city miles away, every small star seemed to sparkle.

There was a quiet there that I hadn't experienced since I was a kid. The smallest rustle of a little animal moving through the woods was audible.

I closed my eyes and listened to the nothingness around me. I'd never thought I'd enjoy it, especially after growing up surrounded by the sounds of the city.

I knew in that moment that I didn't want to leave. The serenity that surrounded me sucked me in, and I couldn't imagine going back to the frigid city with no job in sight.

I pulled my phone out of my pocket and sent a message to Thomas.

Me: We'll talk after the wedding, but I want to hear more about the business.

Staying there would send my mother over the edge, but this was my life to live.

I walked inside and pulled off my clothes before I dropped them on the floor and climbed into bed. I stared at the ceiling and thought about my possible move and new career path.

I'd just have to find a way to break it to my ma. Leaving her behind was something she'd throw in my face for the rest of my life. She'd probably fall at my feet or hang on to my bumper as I drove out of the city, screaming for me not to leave her.

I was sure my imagination was just a tad overactive; she'd wish me well and kiss me goodbye.

Who the hell was I kidding? Fran was gonna have a meltdown.

CHAPTER TWO

MORGAN

Shit-Faced Drunk

Fran was plastered. I mean completely shit-faced. Talking nonstop, smiling more than usual, and smoking like a train.

She'd never been a drinker, but at weddings, something inside her shifted. She'd consume more than her fair share of alcohol and suddenly turn into a chain smoker.

It was the perfect time to drop the news, that I'd be moving, in her lap. Maybe her drunkenness would extend her reaction time and give me a chance to escape before she tried to beat me to death.

That was the thing about her.

She loved me, and often she was overbearing, melodramatic, and fiercely protective. Not only would she beat the crap out of anyone who hurt me, she'd willingly do the same to me if she thought it was for my own good.

No matter how many times Ma had hit me, I'd never thought about striking her back. She'd raised me to respect women, and I knew that, if I ever did raise a hand to her, my uncle would end my life.

21

My size made her ability to actually hurt me impossible, but I knew that it was how she'd react. She wouldn't throw a right hook, but she'd pound on my chest and beg me not to leave. Hopefully, giving her the news at the wedding would stop her from causing a scene.

"Hey, Ma." I pulled out the chair next to her. I glanced at Uncle Sal, who was kicked back and just enjoying life now that his only daughter was married off.

"Hey, baby." She looked up at me with a sloppy smile, a cigarette between her fingers with ash an inch too long hanging from the end. "Whatcha doin'?" she asked as she hiccupped.

"I wanted to talk to you about something." I sat down and pulled my chair close to her.

Uncle Sal cleared his throat, standing quickly. "I'm going to leave you two alone."

"Thanks, Uncle." I nodded.

"Sal." Ma reached out and grabbed his hand. "Be a dear and get me another one of those fruity things." She looked up at him, grinning.

He nodded, patting her hand before he disappeared through the crowd and left us to talk.

I fidgeted with my drink as I thought about how to break the news to her. There wasn't an easy way to say it. I needed to man up and just...

"Just spill it, Morgan." She took a long, slow drag of her cigarette and let the smoke waft out of her mouth.

"I found a job," I blurted out, figuring it was best to lead with something positive.

"Does it have anything to do with those criminals back home?" She rested her elbow on the table, holding the cigarette in the air like an old-school Hollywood actress as the ash tumbled to the plate in front of her.

"No. Thomas actually asked me to come work for him."

A smile crept across her face. "Thank God, honest work. I didn't know he was opening a Chicago branch." She took another drag, almost missing her mouth in the process.

Uncle Sal stood behind her, listening to our conversation. I nodded at him before he set the drink in front of her.

She grabbed the glass and took a sip. "Thank you, brother."

He walked away quickly, knowing that the real bomb hadn't been dropped yet.

"He's not opening an office in Chicago, Ma." I swallowed hard as I looked around the backyard.

Her eyes narrowed. "What do you mean?" She set the drink on the table too hard, causing some of the liquid to slosh out of the glass.

"I'm going to move here as soon as we get back and I pack up my things." I leaned back in the chair and out of arm's reach.

"Move?" she asked, placing her hand on her chest. "You can't move."

"I am." I crossed my arms over my chest, standing my ground.

Here we go.

I braced myself and waited for her to embarrass the hell out of me in front of my entire family. Big Fran was ready to blow.

"You have nowhere to live," she argued.

"I'm going to rent Joe's guesthouse until I find a place."

"You're going to leave me all alone in Chicago?"

There was the guilt trip—right on cue.

"Seriously, Ma. You've been alone for years. I promise to come visit all the time." I knew this was going to be a battle.

"Alone," she whined. "Don't leave me alone." She face-planted on the table, one hand on the drink and the other still holding the cigarette.

If I hadn't been trying to avoid a battle, I'd have laughed. Drunk Ma was funny as hell and kind of cute, although I'd never admit it.

I closed my eyes, took a deep breath, and opened them again. "You have a bunch of friends. You'll be fine."

She sat upright and tapped her cigarette against the ashtray. "If you're moving here, then so am I," she said, looking really happy about the situation.

Oh my God.

No.

She was following me.

I wanted to face-plant now, but instead I took it in an entirely different direction.

I looked up toward the starry sky and cursed under my breath before I said, "That's a great idea, Ma."

Please, please God, tomorrow when the drinks had worn off, make her see the error of her ways.

If she decided to follow me, she'd at least have Uncle Sal and Auntie Mar to keep her busy and out of my hair. Maybe being around the family would take some of the heat off me.

It could end up being a good thing in the end.

What the hell was I thinking? It was going to be a clusterfuck of awesomeness.

"It's settled, then." She stubbed her cigarette out. "When are you going to get married?" she threw at me out of left field.

"I have to find a woman first," I shot back.

"You're getting old, baby. Don't wait too long, or you'll be alone forever."

"Hold up, woman." I held my hand up, shushing her. "Look around. Joe was older when he married. All of my cousins were older than I am now when they found love and settled down."

"Not Izzy," she replied, pursing her lips.

"Izzy's a girl."

"So? I want to be a grandmother before I'm dead."

There it was. The baby topic. I had known it was coming. Being around the kids all week had put her in baby mode.

How freaking lucky was I?

I swear she'd been dying since I was a kid. Every time she wanted to get her way, she'd talk about how her end was near.

"It'll be years before I have a kid. I'm not ready. So you'll have to hold off on dying."

"I just look around and see how happy Sal and Mar are with their grandbabies, and it makes my womb ache."

"Then maybe you should adopt. Think of all the fun and happiness you could have raising another child."

Never mind the fact that she'd have someone else to pester all the time.

"You were enough to last a lifetime. You weren't the easiest child to raise."

"Womb isn't aching that bad, is it?" I teased her.

"Everything okay?" Auntie Mar mouthed as she approached the table.

I nodded to her. "Hey, Auntie Mar. I just told Ma that I'm moving to Florida."

"Oh." She tried to act surprised. "Are you okay, Frannie?" Aunt Mar sat down next to her, placing her hand on Ma's arm.

"I couldn't be better, Maria. I've decided I'm going to move here too. I've spent too long away from you guys." Ma laid her hand over Aunt Mar's, both women plastered but sharing a moment.

"That makes me a happy woman. Sunday dinners at my house just got a whole lot more fun," Aunt Mar sang, swaying in her chair.

"We wouldn't miss it for the world," Ma answered for us both.

Normally it would have pissed me off, but I loved Aunt Mar's food too much to ever miss out on a Sunday dinner, and Ma was just too damn drunk to be angry with her.

"Are you two enjoying the wedding?" Aunt Mar glanced around the backyard.

"It was a beautiful ceremony, and the yard looks amazing," Ma said as she skimmed the crowd, trying to focus.

It really did look spectacular. Tables lined the perimeter of the grass, with a dance floor in the center. Lanterns and candles illuminated the backyard, creating a warm glow for the guests. Everyone seemed to be having a great time; most people were sufficiently drunk by now anyway.

"It's been a busy few days, but everything turned out perfectly," Aunt Mar replied.

"Izzy has turned into quite the beauty. You have to be so proud of her." Ma's eyes landed on Izzy, who was on the dance floor, dancing in her father's arms.

"She was the hardest of my children to raise. She's so full of piss and vinegar, and naturally the last to get married."

"She's like you, Mar. Headstrong and tough."

"Well, ladies, I'm going to let you two gab a bit while I find my cousins."

"They're at the bar," my aunt replied as I stood.

"Perfect." I leaned down and gave them each a kiss on the cheek.

As I started to walk away, Aunt Mar asked, "Does he have a girlfriend?"

"No, and he isn't getting any younger, either," Ma complained as her voice trailed off.

I shook the insult off. I wasn't even thirty yet and they wanted me to settle down. The last thing I was thinking about now was a relationship.

Winding my way through the crowd, I spotted Thomas and James at the bar doing shots.

"Gentlemen," I said as I approached. "Care if I join you?"

"Have a drink." James held a shot glass out. "Let's celebrate."

"Thanks. What are we drinking to?" I took the shot from his hands.

"The future." Thomas raised his glass. "Both in love and success in work."

"I'll drink to that."

"Thinking about joining us?" James asked.

"I put some thought into it and I've decided I want to work for you. I love Florida, and I'm sick of the shitty weather in Chicago anyway. I'd like to give it a try."

"Fantastic." Thomas pumped his fist. "Let's drink to another important member of our team. We're going to kick some major ass, men." He held his glass high in the air as we tapped ours to his and drank.

I winced as the liquid slid down my throat, burning a path to my stomach. "What the hell was that?"

"Moonshine." James wiped his mouth with the back of his hand.

"Fuck," I coughed, trying to fill my lungs with air as my throat felt like it was closing.

"It'll wear off." James slapped me on the back.

I coughed again, trying to clear my throat, but with no luck. I swallowed it down, trying to cool the burn with my saliva.

"Another?" James asked with a cocky grin and a raised eyebrow.

"I think I'll stick with vodka. It's a bit smoother," I whispered.

"Pussy." James called over to the bartender. "We'll take a bottle of vodka."

"A bottle, sir?" the man asked with a perplexed look on his face.

James nodded, holding his hand out. "Yes. The entire bottle and six shot glasses."

"It's going to be one of those nights, isn't it?" I realized I'd probably have a pounding headache tomorrow. "Do you want to be drunk on your wedding night?"

"It's going to take more than splitting a bottle of vodka with the guys to get me drunk." He grabbed the bottle, leaving us standing there.

"Okay, then," I said to Thomas as we grabbed the shot glasses and followed James toward a table where Joe, Mike, and Anthony were sitting.

"Hey, boys." James placed the bottle in the center of the table. "It's time to celebrate."

Joe pulled his bow tie off and tossed it before cracking his neck. "Finally. Is it after ten yet?"

"Yeah, dude. It's way after ten," Anthony answered.

"Thank fuck," Joe mumbled. "Pour me a shot."

"What the hell does ten have to do with anything?" I was completely confused.

"Ma made us all promise not to have more than two drinks before ten," Joe replied. "None of us felt like hearing her bullshit if we didn't follow her rules."

"Mothers."

"They're a pisser." James grabbed the bottle and poured us each a shot.

We toasted to various things, drinking shot after shot until the bottle was empty. I listened to my cousins talk. They'd never been so happy in their entire lives.

I didn't know if I'd ever feel that way. Finding a woman who was willing to put up with my shit would be a difficult endeavor. I hadn't given up on love, but I didn't think I was ready.

For now, I'd bury myself in my work and enjoy learning the Floridian way of life. Everything there, and it would take some getting used to.

The rest of the evening breezed by. We danced and drank until most of the guests left. When I'd had enough, I found Ma still sipping on a "fruity drink." She was too drunk to care.

"Night, baby," she slurred.

"Night, Ma. Love you." I gave her a kiss.

"Love you too," she whispered.

I wandered to the front yard and grabbed a taxi. Auntie Mar, in all of her wisdom, had hired a horde of them to take guests home who were too smashed to drive home.

Tomorrow was a new beginning. I'd make a plan and meet with Thomas at the office while James and Izzy jetted off to their honeymoon.

Life was looking up, and change was on the horizon.

CHAPTER THREE

MORGAN

Sunshine

It wasn't hard to say goodbye to Chicago. After I served in the army, it didn't feel like home anymore. It took me a week to gather my things and head south.

Four days after I'd arrived in Florida with all of my belongings in tow and passed the exam for my Florida PI license, I was ready for my first day of work.

I stopped in front of the doorway to ALFA PI and cracked my neck, shaking my hands to calm my nerves. Even though my cousin owned the company, I didn't want to fuck shit up.

When I pushed the door open, Angel had the phone resting on her shoulder as she jotted down a note.

"I'll have Mr. Gallo call you as soon as his meeting is over, sir." She held a finger up.

The wall behind her desk had the company logo with the words *Aggressive-Loyal-Fearless-Accurate* inscribed underneath. I stared at it for a moment before taking in the rest of the office. Modern interior, gray and black walls, and not a knickknack or file visible. Sunlight streamed in from the wall of windows that comprised the eastern side of the building.

"Hey, Morgan," Angel said as she hung up. "Thomas is expecting you, and I'm excited to have you here."

"Thanks, Angel. I hope my cousin is happy too."

She smiled, rising from her seat. "Oh, he is. They've been so busy we've had to turn away cases. I know they sure could use your help." She motioned for me to follow. "Let me show you to his office."

As we walked down a hallway, a door caught my eye and I stopped.

It read:

Morgan DeLuca
Intelligence Services & Surveillance Specialist

I couldn't help but feel my insides warm.

"I told you he's happy to have you," she whispered.

"I guess so." I grinned.

Angel touched my arm, breaking my trance. "Come on. You can check your office out after you talk with the boss." She knocked lightly before entering.

"We'll see you tomorrow." Thomas put his feet down. "Morgan is here. I'll catch ya later. Glad you're back, man."

"Thomas." I walked toward him.

He tossed his cell phone on top of the desk, letting it bounce. He rose to his feet and came around the desk. "It's good to see you. That was James." He shook my hand. "He'll be in tomorrow."

"I heard."

"Hey, beautiful." He extended his arm to Angel.

She walked to him, snuggled into his side, and kissed his jaw. "You want any coffee or anything, baby?" She looked up at him with a small smile.

"No, thanks, love. Morgan?" he asked before he kissed her head.

"No, thanks. I'm good." I took a seat across from my new boss.

One thing I noticed with the Gallo men: They held their women close and often showered them with kisses. I envied them, but I'd never admit it.

Angel walked out, closing the door behind her as Thomas sat back down and I looked around the office.

"See your new office?" He put his feet back up on the desk, resting his hands behind his head.

I nodded. "I did. Thanks, man. It was beyond cool seeing that."

"You came at the perfect time. We hadn't even thought about you until I heard you were coming to the wedding. I did your background check before you arrived."

"Isn't that illegal?"

"I have friends who helped me work around the legalities. That's part of this job. Sometimes we're on the fringe of breaking laws. I assume you don't have any problem with that?" he asked with a raised eyebrow.

I shook my head. "Never been an issue for me before. I don't know why it would be now."

"Sometimes when we have to get information, we use all means necessary."

"Am I going to be stuck in that office all day?" I wondered if my job title meant "trapped in front of a computer screen."

"Hell no. God, that would be horrible. You're going to be going out on jobs like the rest of us. What I had put on your door is your specialty."

"Gotcha." I relaxed a little into the chair.

"I already have a case picked out for you, if you're willing to start as soon as possible."

"I'm all yours."

I was ready.

I'd never been the type for idleness, and after having been home for over a month, I wanted nothing more than to dive headfirst into my first case.

I was now Morgan, P.I. More handsome than Magnum, and hopefully, I'd do a better job at solving the cases. Maybe I should have grabbed myself one of those flowery shirts he always wore on television. Nah, I'd look like a giant douche. I liked my classic style of blue jeans and T-shirts.

He shuffled through the files on his desk and pulled one out. "Here she is. Her name is Race True." He handed it to me. "She came in a couple of days ago."

I opened the folder and scanned the first page. "What's her situation?"

"I don't have the entire story. She stated she'd only divulge it to the PI working her case. Basically, she's been getting harassed, and the messages have become more aggressive."

"Oh." I read through her questionnaire.

Thomas's phone rang and I continued reading as he began speaking with a client.

Race True was a twenty-seven-year-old woman who worked as a senior contract manager at a downtown communications firm. She'd lived in the Tampa area her entire life, except when she'd attended NYU. She held a master's degree in business and lived on her own in Clearwater. Not too much information, but at least it narrowed our possible suspects down.

I rested the file on my leg and stared out the window. What could have had this girl jumpy enough about an e-mail to cause her to seek help? Why not just go to the police, report the situation, and let them follow up on the threats?

Thomas rubbed his forehead as he hung up the phone.

"What's wrong?" I studied his face.

"Just bullshit from a case I worked on last week. It's a wife who suspected her husband of cheating. Long story. What do you think of Race?" he asked as he fidgeted in his chair, rocking back and forth.

"Not too much to go on."

He nodded, setting his lips in a firm line. "I know. Why don't I show you to your office, tell you a little bit about our rules, and then you can set up a meeting with her?"

I closed her file and stood. "I want to get working right away."

"Then let's get you settled," he said as he rose from his chair and walked around the desk. As he slapped me on the back, he said, "Welcome to the team, Morgan."

"It's good to be part of something again."

"Ms. True, please," I said to the woman on the other end of the line.

"This is she. With whom am I speaking?" she asked in the sexiest Southern voice I'd ever heard.

"Morgan DeLuca from ALFA P.I. I was given your case, ma'am."

She hissed loud enough for it to catch me off guard. "I hate being called that."

I made a quick mental note not to make that mistake again. "Sorry." I gritted my teeth. "Just trying to be polite, Ms. True."

"It's fine. So, you're my guy?"

"Yes. I'd like to schedule a meeting to discuss the details you left off your questionnaire."

"Ah. If you're going to be working for me, then I'll share them with you, but no one else."

"That's fine." I tapped the pencil against my desktop. "When are you available?"

"I can meet you tomorrow for lunch. Let's say noon at the Blue Martini. Do you know where that is?"

"Yes," I lied. "I'll be there at noon." I'd lived here for a total of ninety-six hours, but I'd find it without trouble.

"Mr. DeLuca." She cleared her throat. "Please be prompt. I don't have time to waste waiting around for you."

"Yes, ma'am," I replied before hanging up. I grimaced, knowing she'd probably cursed me because I'd called her that again.

I leaned back in my chair, taking in my new digs. The walls matched the gray ones in the waiting room. On the opposite wall from my desk there was a modern black leather couch, and two chairs were immediately in front of my desk.

My eyes stung from the endless hours of staring at a computer, trying to learn the new programs. I climbed to my feet and stretched before I grabbed my keys. I looked around my office, finally letting it sink in. I had a new purpose and could start a brand-new life. Wanting to say goodbye to Thomas, I headed to his office before leaving.

"Hey." I opened the door and froze, seeing more than I expected.

Thomas had Angel bent over the desk with her skirt pulled up and was banging the hell out of her.

Their eyes met mine as I stood in the doorway, unable to move. "Sorry." I finally found my footing and took a step backward. I closed the door and took a deep breath. "Fuck," I muttered as I looked up at the ceiling. "I'll be back later!"

"Take the afternoon off!" Thomas yelled back.

"Thanks." I had to look like a kid who'd walked in on his parents.

Since I was diving right into work, I figured I'd better get my ass home, my car unpacked, and settle in.

I planned to be there for a very long time.

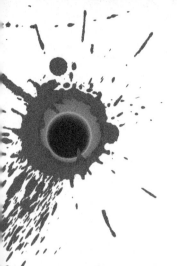

CHAPTER FOUR

MORGAN

Hottie in Heels

I overslept and missed my workout. I had to haul ass to make it on time to the Blue Martini. I texted Thomas in the morning, still slightly embarrassed, and told him I'd be in the office after my meeting with Ms. True.

Walking toward the restaurant, I peered down at my clothes, feeling out of place. While the rest of the crowd was wearing suits and business casual, I had my usual jeans and T-shirt on.

I stood in the doorway, surveying the bar and trying to pick Ms. True out of the crowd.

A woman peered up from her phone and looked back down.

Whoever she was, she was fucking gorgeous. She sat there with her spine straight, blond hair in a perfect bun, and a crisp black dress shirt tucked into a gray pencil skirt. Her high cheekbones almost kissed her deep-green eyes.

I wanted to saunter up to her, ask her for her number, and beg that on our first date she wear the red stilettos she had on, which made my cock instantly hard.

She glanced up, caught me staring, and waved me over.

Well, hell. Maybe she wanted my number too.

Keep calm and act natural.

Her eyes remained down, concentrating on her phone, as I approached.

"Mr. DeLuca, I presume." She glanced up for a moment, her emerald eyes flickering. "Take a seat."

Disappointment flooded me. The beautiful creature in front of me wasn't calling me over to get my number. She was my new client.

"Ms. True?" I let my eyes linger on her legs for a little too long but not caring.

"Yes," she said, still not making eye contact.

I grabbed the small pad of paper and pen I'd jammed in my back pocket and tossed them on the bar. "I hope you don't mind if I take notes." I tried not to stare at her legs, but failed.

"I do, actually." She dropped the phone in her purse, pinning me with her fierce, green eyes. "I'd prefer if you remember everything I tell you. I don't want a paper trail." The look on my face had to be one of total confusion, because she added, "I don't want anything possibly getting into the wrong hands."

"Okay."

"Good. Let's order and then we'll talk." She snapped her fingers to get the bartender's attention. "Do you know what you want?"

"Yeah. I come here all the time," I lied.

When the waitress approached, Race placed her order filled with special requests. She didn't like tomatoes but wanted extra cheese and only wanted grilled chicken.

I learned within five minutes that Race True wasn't easy. She seemed uptight, controlled, and unwilling to bend.

"And you, sir?" the beautiful bartender asked.

"Just a water, please."

"That's it? No giant, sloppy burger?" Ms. True asked, blinking rapidly.

"That's it." I glanced between them.

Race shrugged and waited for the bartender to reach the far end of the bar before she started to speak. "I thought I'd buy you lunch while we talked."

"I'd rather keep this strictly professional, Ms. True."

Lie number three.

I did want to be professional, but sitting here and staring at her had my mind going a million different ways, and most of them were sexual.

Fuck. I needed to get laid or everything could derail in a hurry. Why couldn't she have been unattractive? As I watched her, I wanted to know if she was as difficult to please in bed as she was at having a simple meal. I wondered if she screamed when she was fucked or what her hair looked like when her bun was taken down.

Race had pouty red lips, the whitest teeth I'd ever seen on a human being other than movie stars, and eyes the shade of emeralds. She was average size, with fabulous tits that peeked out from the neckline of her blouse and drew my attention. The pencil skirt accentuated her hips and made her legs seem a mile long.

"So, Morgan. Tell me a little bit about your background before I tell you about my problem. I want to know that you're the right man for the job." She sipped her wine, keeping her green eyes pinned on me.

It wasn't going to be easy to keep my thoughts from straying from the purpose of the meeting. Hopefully, our contact would be minimal and mainly over the phone so I wouldn't have to risk a slap in the face from gawking at her tits.

"I recently left the army after serving eight years. I worked the last four years gathering intel for the troops on the battlefield."

"Oh," she interrupted, placing the glass on the bar and resting her hand near mine. "That's impressive."

"Not really, ma'am."

She stiffened and rubbed the bridge of her nose.

"Sorry. It's a military thing. Everyone is a ma'am or a sir. It has nothing to do with me thinking you're anything like your grandmother, but I'm sure she's a lovely woman."

"She's a conniving hag. I'm nothing like her."

"Got it."

"Continue." She grabbed her glass again, averting her eyes.

"I became a civilian again about a month ago."

"What makes Mr. Gallo so sure you're the right man for the job?" she questioned, eyeing me with speculation.

I turned to face her, resting my arm on the bar. I didn't like that I had to defend my qualifications to her. "Listen, Ms. True. If you're not comfortable with me working your case, I can ask for someone else to be assigned to you. Right now, we don't have the manpower for another investigator to take over right away. If you're willing to wait, I'm sure we can find you a more suitable replacement. Someone more to your...liking. But no one will work as hard as I will."

"No." Her voice was louder than before. "I just need to have someone work on this case who knows their shit. I can't have some hack trying to clear my good name and fuck shit up." Her jaw clenched as she pinned me with her stare.

My dick twitched—honest to God, moved inside my pants from her filthy mouth.

"As long as you can promise me that you have the skills I need to find out who's behind this, then you're my guy." She placed her hand on my arm.

I smirked, feeling a bit playful. "I have the skills you desire." I glanced down, feeling the coolness of her touch on my warm skin. "I'm your man. I have more training in intelligence gathering than anyone else in my office. I was trained by the best the military had to offer. I have no doubt I'll find the perpetrator."

She nodded, brushing her fingertips across my skin before removing her hand slowly. "Fine. I'm sorry if I came off bitchy there for a moment. I know you're new. You weren't there when I went to the office to seek help. I just want to make sure I don't have the newbie who's learning on the job."

"Why don't you tell me about what's going on? Your file lacked anything to help me start identifying my plan of attack. I promise you this, Ms. True: I'll give your case my full attention and the utmost privacy."

She glanced around the bar, checking our surroundings. "The messages started about a year ago. First they were just strange. You know, the type you delete and forget about." She waved her hands in the air near her shoulder. "But then," she whispered as her eyes grew large, "then the person started mentioning personal stuff that only someone I knew would know."

"Like what type of details?"

"I wasn't always this put-together lady you see in front of you today." She fidgeted. "I made questionable decisions in college."

"That's part of the college experience," I said in a soothing tone. "You were a normal kid. Do you know anyone from college who would want to cause you harm?" I tapped the pen against the paper, wishing I could take notes.

She shook her head, slowly bringing her eyes to mine. "Not that I can think of, but obviously, there's someone." She said the last word with a look that let me know she thought I wasn't the brightest light bulb in the fixture.

"I promise I'll find the person." I dropped the pen on the paper. "I'll need access to your e-mail or any other means of communication they've used to reach you. Also, I'll need you to make a list of your known associates from college."

"I don't know." Her eyes shifted.

"Listen, Ms. True. The only thing that matters to me is solving your case and having you walk away satisfied."

She stared at me as her lips parted.

I cleared my throat, shifting in my seat. "A satisfied customer. That's what I meant." I settled back in my chair and smirked.

She swallowed hard as her eyes dipped to my hands. "Fine, Morgan."

Not only did her attitude ooze from her body, it slipped from her lips like it was part of her. There wasn't one piece of her that didn't exude class or social status. I was the grunt in this situation, and she didn't let that fact slide.

"I'll gather the information for you and have it delivered to your office," Race said as she looked back up at the motion of the approaching server.

The bartender placed Race's meal in front of her and asked if I wanted anything, but I waved her off.

"If you trust someone enough to bring it on your behalf." I stood, not letting her off the hook so easily.

"Fuck," she whispered. "I don't. I'll bring it to your office in a day or so. Where are you going?" She pursed her lips.

"I gotta get back to the office. You enjoy your lunch, Ms. True." I threw enough to cover the bill on the bar. "I look forward to working with you."

"I'll see you in a couple of days, Mr. DeLuca, but I'm more than capable of paying for my own lunch."

Jesus, she was a stubborn.

"I know, but I got it." I didn't add anything else as I started to stride away. "See you in a couple of days, Race," I said over my shoulder, taking in her beauty one more time.

Race True was used to getting her way.

I'd take every chance to remind her that I was in charge of this investigation. I might have been working on her behalf, but shit was going to go down the way I wanted it to go.

If I failed, her life could be ruined and I could be out of a job before I'd even started.

CHAPTER FIVE

RACE

Secrets

For two days, I thought about nothing but *him*.

Morgan DeLuca was a cocky son of a bitch, but it didn't stop me from fantasizing about him. He was a bossy prick. I knew the type from working in the corporate world, but Morgan had a kindness in his eyes. I couldn't forget his face. His distinctive features would be forever etched in my brain. I don't mean just a guy I'd give a second look to when walking by.

He had the package.

Strong, chiseled face lined with dark stubble. Lips so full that I'd feel them long after a kiss had ended, muscles that bulged from places that shouldn't be legal, and eyes so blue that I could get lost in them for hours.

Oh, seriously.

I needed to get a fucking grip. It wasn't like it had been that long since I'd had sex.

Had it?

I'd been too busy trying to climb the corporate ladder to even bother with any type of relationship. Plus, the men I worked with just didn't do it for me. I liked them rough around the edges with a hint of beautiful underneath.

Like Morgan.

I walked into his office two days later with an envelope filled with possible suspects, copies of the e-mails, and other information I thought he needed.

Their receptionist spoke on the phone as I tapped my fingernails against the desk, waiting for her.

She kept holding up her finger. I looked at my watch, wondering how long I'd have to stand here.

She was a pretty little thing with long red hair that flowed over her shoulders. I hadn't paid much attention to her when I had been there the first time. Maybe she was Morgan's type—pretty and perky, with a natural beauty and casual attire.

"Sorry, ma'am. Can I help you?" she asked as she hung up the phone.

I righted myself, trying not to feel a pang of jealousy. "I'm here to see Mr. DeLuca."

"And you are?" Her eyes raked over my upper body.

Oh my God. Was she checking me out like I had her?

"Ms. True," I said with an overly sweet voice.

She pushed back from the desk, popped up from her seat, and left me alone in the waiting room.

Moments later, she returned with Morgan following close behind her.

"Ah, Race."

"Ms. True," I corrected him, pushing my shoulder back.

His eyes dropped to my chest as he smirked. "Let's talk in my office where it's more... private."

I followed him to his office, staring at his ass as we walked. When he held the door open, he barely left me enough space to pass by without touching him.

46

My shoulder brushed against his and his scent hit me. I closed my eyes, taking in the rich cologne he was wearing, trying to memorize it.

"Please sit." He pushed the door closed with his body.

I fidgeted with the envelope as he sat across from me, leaning back in his chair. He looked handsome today, but the stubble on his jaw had disappeared.

Pity, really, because I liked how it had looked.

He placed his hands flat on the desk as he sat. "What did you bring for me?"

I blinked twice, clearing my mind before I tossed the envelope on the desk, not trusting my voice.

He glanced down. "Did you bring everything I told you to?" He eyed me.

"Yes. It's my e-mails, including the first message I received. I erased it right after I printed it," I said, feeling foolish, tugging on the edge of my skirt.

"Why don't you tell me what it says?" He cocked his head to the side as he held the envelope without opening it.

I grimaced, squirming in my seat. "It's embarrassing, Mr. DeLuca."

"I don't care what it is. I'm not here to judge you. It would help if I knew what the real issue is. What the hell does this person have on you that is freaking you out so bad?"

Covering my face with my hands, I dug my index fingers into the corners of my eyes. "Oh, God," I whispered, trying to breathe through my nose.

"I promise not to laugh," he said in a steady, calm voice.

"I wish it were funny," I mumbled as my stomach started to knot and my eyes met his.

"Did you sell drugs?" The side of his jaw ticked.

I blinked rapidly at him. "Are you kidding me?"

He shrugged. "No. I'm just trying to come up with what the hell it could possibly be." He rubbed his chin, studying me. "Did you cheat?"

"No." I shook my head, absently stroking my throat.

"Get pregnant and not have the baby?" He raised an eyebrow.

"No. Jesus," I muttered, shaking my head.

"Let's start with something easier. What did the first e-mail say and why did you erase it?" He crossed his arms over his chest.

"I thought it was bullshit. So I just erased it and pretended it never happened." My chest tightened as I peered up at him. "Promise me you won't judge me?" I winced.

"Just spill it, Race. I won't think differently of you, unless you killed someone. We all have a checkered past."

I looked down at my lap. "I was seeing this guy for about a year. I thought we were in love." My stomach churned just from thinking about him.

"And?"

"One night we were partying and—God, this is so stupid." I shook my head, covering my face with my hands. "He convinced me to make a sex video as a memento of our time together."

"That's it?" he said. "It's nothing to be ashamed of."

I dropped my hands as I straightened. "But how many people get a threat that it would be sent to their boss?"

He slapped the desk. "Why didn't you tell me that? It's simple. Has to be your ex-boyfriend."

I shook my head, pursing my lips. "Nope. It's not him. He died after we graduated. But someone claims to have the video." I gave a long, low sigh.

"It's just a job, Race."

Rubbing my temples, I lifted my head to meet his gaze. "It's all I have, Morgan. I worked my ass off to get where I am today. There's no way in hell I'm going to let anyone destroy it."

"Hmm," he muttered, rubbing his chin. "Okay. It has to be someone who had access to your ex's things after he died. Tell me more about him."

"He was an engineering major, and we met sophomore year. Things between us heated up quickly, and we spent every waking minute together before we broke up at the end of my junior year."

He stared at me for a moment without speaking, continuing to stroke his chin. "Keep going."

"His name was Shane. I bumped into him one day while he was waiting for his cousin after class." I glanced out the office window, thinking about how much easier my life had been then.

"Do you remember his cousin's name?"

I shook my head, looking up at the ceiling. "They weren't close. His cousin was a jerk. I want to say it was something like Kyle or Tyler." I shrugged.

"It's a start, princess."

"I'm really sorry." I blew out a heavy breath. "I wish I could tell you more, but I never spoke to the guy."

"What happened with Shane? Maybe it'll help tie everything together."

I dragged my eyes to him. "I caught him in bed with my best friend. We ended that night. He was the last boyfriend I ever had. Is that good enough?" My cheeks heated as I averted my eyes.

"What a bastard," he growled. "It's okay. I'll see what we can dig up. What was Shane's last name?" he asked, grabbing his cell phone off his desk.

"McGovern."

"Hey, Thomas," Morgan said as he put the phone on his shoulder. "I need you to do some digging if you have time today, or put one of the other guys on it."

His eyes darted to mine. "Yeah. Race just told me about a possible lead. Dig in to Shane McGovern. He's deceased, but I think his cousin has something to do with the threats."

I thought Shane was a nice guy.

I thought he was the one.

It had been six years, and I still hadn't allowed myself to get involved with anyone. My ability to trust had been completely shattered.

"His name is Tyler or Kyle."

I stared at him as he spoke, taking a good look at him without being bombarded with questions.

His muscles bulged underneath the sleeves of the clean white dress shirt, which were rolled up, resting against the middle of his forearms. The top of his hair was longer than the sides, a little grown out since his time in the military. The strands were brown in color but verging on black, with each strand in place.

"You okay?"

"Yeah." I drew my knees together and dragged my eyes to his face. "Sorry. I was thinking about work. What did you ask?"

"I need your account information. I have copies of the e-mails, but the original messages hold information that's critical to tracking the source."

I sank into the chair, crossing my legs. "I don't give that out to anyone." God, I needed to get laid, or else I'd be squeezing my legs together every time I met with him.

He crossed his arms, narrowing his eyes. "I'm not just anyone."

I swallowed hard, wishing he'd been an ugly man closer to sixty instead of the man sitting in front of me. "Sorry. My mind is just elsewhere."

"Haven't we been over this before? I need the information." He leaned forward, clasping his hands together as he rested them on the desk. "Why bother hiring me if you won't trust me enough to do my job?"

"I'm sorry I'm being so difficult." I shifted in my chair, feeling both horny as hell and uncomfortable.

He clenched his jaw. "I just want to help you."

"I know. I'm sorry."

I never usually apologized for my behavior, but with him it was starting to become the norm.

I'd honed my bitch skills right after college.

I'd had to.

I'd walked into work the first day filled with happiness and feeling perkier than ever. I'd landed my dream job and was beyond excited. The cold reality of corporate America had slapped me in the face within five minutes.

From that day forward, I'd put on my best resting bitch face and perfected my go-fuck-yourself stare. I'd never let anyone treat me that way again. I'd become the woman I was that day in Morgan's office. Confident and powerful, and nothing in the world would make me change, including the cocksucker who was trying to blackmail me.

"I promise I will only look at the e-mails that pertain to your case. Your privacy is very important to me, Race." He spoke in a soothing tone.

I nodded, scooted forward in the chair, and grabbed a pen. On a piece of scrap paper that was lying nearby, I wrote down my e-mail log-in information and the website address he'd need to access the account. "Here." I pushed it toward him, giving him a weak smile.

"Was that so hard?"

I tilted my head to the side. "Be careful, Mr. DeLuca. I can still fire you."

"But you won't." He smirked.

I bit my lip, holding back the comment that sat on the edge of my tongue. I stood quickly, smoothing my skirt. "Call me when you figure out who's sending the messages, and I'll handle it from there."

He hopped to his feet and came around the desk before I made it to the door. "Once I have the name, I'll be in contact and *we'll* decide together the best course of action."

I stared up at him, my nostrils flaring. God, he smelled so good. I wanted to rub against him and find out if his entire body was as hard as it looked.

I had to snap out of it.

This is business, Race.

"Race?" He touched my arm.

I jerked my arm away. "Call me once you have a name and we'll discuss it then," I replied, backing up and bumping into the chair with the backs of my knees. I cleared my throat. "Damn," I mumbled.

"Would you like me to show you out?"

"No," I answered, wanting to put some distance between us. I needed to. "Thank you. I know the way." I turned around, warmth creeping up my chest and neck.

He'd turned me into a clumsy idiot.

"I'll see you soon, Race," he called as I walked out.

I didn't turn around as I closed the door. Then collapsed against it as I bowed my head.

"You okay out there?" he yelled from the other side of the door.

I winced, feeling lightheaded. "Just checking my messages!" I yelled. I pushed off the door and practically jogged out of the building.

When I walked outside, I could smell him still.

Damn it.

I'd have to spend the entire day smelling him, and it would be wasted with fantasies of Morgan DeLuca and his powerful body mingling with mine as I surrendered all control to him.

God, I was so fucked that it wasn't even funny.

I needed to get to the gym and run off some of the pent-up energy. Being near him had me feel something that I didn't like to feel.

Vulnerable.

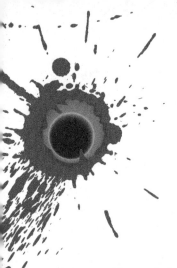

CHAPTER SIX

MORGAN

The Weekend

It was early, and the sun still hung low as it streamed through the trees, casting shadows on the grass. Standing outside, I watched a wild turkey walk through the backyard as I sipped on a cup of coffee and thought about my day.

I went through a checklist of shit I needed to get accomplished. The top of my list: Race True.

It had been a week since our last meeting. I wanted to let her know that I had made headway in her case. I'd e-mailed her last night asking her to meet me tonight.

There were a few assumptions I'd made about Race during our two interactions. She didn't like to be bossed around, but I wondered if there was ever a time she gave up her control.

Race acted like she didn't like me much, but I could tell that she did. I'd caught her more times than I could count checking me out.

No matter what came out of her mouth, I knew that her attraction to me was as great as mine was to her.

She was strong, independent, and self-assured, but there was more to her. Something sweet and kind that had been tamped down over time was hidden under the surface.

Something inside me wanted to find out.

Plus, I needed a little fun. I lived in the sticks, and there wasn't a damn thing to do around here. The last thing I wanted to do tonight was sit by the fire and watch the stars pass overhead again.

I figured I'd meet with Race and see where the night took us. I wanted to dig deeper and find out what made her tick.

My phone chimed as I dumped my coffee into the sink, ready to start the day.

Race: I'll be there at 5 sharp. Don't keep me waiting.

I stared at the screen. I'd been waiting since I'd seen her a week ago. The real Race True would reveal herself tonight.

As I climbed into my car, I replied.

Me: Change of plans. Meet me at the Fly Bar around 5. I'll be waiting for you.

I tossed my phone on the passenger seat, revved the engine, and turned the radio up before I pulled away.

I could tell that this was going to be a kickass day and the best way to start the weekend.

Thomas tossed a file onto his desk. "We need to hire someone else," he told James, avoiding eye contact.

James nodded, collapsing on the couch. "You're right. Any ideas who?"

"I don't know." Thomas dragged his hands through his hair.

"Morgan, you know anyone?" James asked.

I shook my head. "I don't know anyone around here."

"The only person I can think of is..." Thomas started, rubbing his chin.

"Don't." James waved him off.

Thomas slapped the desk, glaring at James. "Come on, man. So much time has passed. She's your wife now, for shit's sake."

"You know I don't like him, Thomas." James wrinkled his nose.

"James, get the fuck over it already. Sam and Izzy are only friends. She's in love with you, and Sam has a woman."

"How do you know?" James sat up.

Thomas kicked his feet up on the desk and reclined in his chair. "We've been in contact."

I looked between them both as they stared each other down. "Um, who the fuck is Sam?"

Thomas glanced at me. "Izzy's friend," he replied.

"Her old fuck buddy," James said, curling his lip.

"Oh." My mouth fell open.

"I'll never forgive him for putting her in danger, Thomas."

Thomas nodded, placing his hands behind his head. "I know, but we wouldn't have been able to save Angel and Izzy without him."

"We wouldn't have had to rescue Izzy if it weren't for his dumb ass."

Thomas glared at James. "You wouldn't be married to Izzy if it weren't for his mistake."

A small smile crept across James's face as he puffed his chest out. "True," he said as his cheeks filled before he blew out a long breath. "I hadn't thought about it that way."

"Stop being such an asshole all the time. Sam has the qualifications, and from what I can tell from his e-mails, he's not enjoying life in the Big Easy that much." Thomas rocked back and forth as he stared at the ceiling.

I glanced down at my watch. I had one hour until I had to meet Race. The minutes seemed to slow the later in the day it became.

"You said he's found a woman?" James asked with a wrinkled brow.

"Yeah. He said he's never been so in love. Her name's Fiona, and she's a nurse in the city."

"Hmm," James muttered. "Good to know he's moved on."

"Are you threatened by him? Think Izzy would leave you for him?" Thomas teased.

"No. Izzy loves me. She knows I'd never let her go without a fight."

Thomas glanced at him, giving him the evil eye. "If my sister wanted to leave you, I'd make sure she got her way. Remember, I'll always take my sister's side."

"You know I would never hurt her. I love the woman."

"I'm just sayin'. I love you like a brother, but she'll always be my sister."

"Thomas." James threw a ball of paper at him. "I wouldn't expect anything less."

"So, are we okay with Sam?" Thomas asked, his face softening.

"If you think we need him."

I pulled another file from the stack, ignoring their conversation. Maybe a little work would make the minutes tick by quicker.

"We do. He'll be a great addition to the team. Trust me. He's over Izzy."

"If you say so. I think Sam and I will have a little chat," James said, balling up another piece of paper.

"I'm sure everyone will want to have a little talk with him."

"You know that everyone may have a coronary if you invite him to be part of this business."

Thomas shook his head, rolling his eyes much like Izzy often did. "Dude, they'll get the fuck over it just like you."

James laughed. "Yeah. I'm sure they will," he said, tossing the paper ball in the air and catching it again. "Make the call and see if you can get him back here, then."

"I'll call him over the weekend. I told Angel I'd take her to dinner tonight. We're making Friday our date night."

"Aww, that's so sweet it makes my teeth hurt," James teased, smirking at Thomas.

"What are you doing tonight?" Thomas asked him, changing the subject. "Izzy is probably dying to go out."

"Oh, we have plans. We're hitting the club tonight."

I looked up and caught Thomas glaring at James with his lips set in a firm line.

"James." Thomas sat upright in the chair as his body grew rigid. "I told you I don't want to know a damn thing about it. Didn't I make myself clear?"

"Sometimes it sucks being married to your sister. I can never share the good stuff with you," James complained with a pained expression.

"You better not be sharing the *good stuff* with anyone," Thomas replied, not taking his eyes off James.

"What club?" I asked, interrupting their conversation.

Maybe I could get Race to head over there after the bar tonight. I'd love to see if she could dance. I hadn't been to a nightclub since I was too young to drink.

I missed so much shit from having been away for eight years.

"It's not your type of club." Thomas's eyes slowly moved to mine.

"What type of club is it?"

James chuckled. "It's not a nightclub."

"A strip club?" I asked, raising an eyebrow.

"Nope," James said in a clipped tone.

"I'm lost. Swingers club?" I turned around to face him fully. "Tell me you don't have my cousin sleeping with random dudes?"

"I'd never let anyone touch her but me," James glanced at me before glaring at Thomas.

"Then what? Can someone clue me the fuck in?"

James laughed louder. "Why don't I walk you out and I'll tell you. Thomas gets kind of testy when I talk about it." James rolled off the couch, climbing to his feet.

"Sure, man."

"Fucker," Thomas hissed.

"Dude, get the fuck over it, as you said earlier." James walked toward the door.

Thomas glared at James's back as his nostrils flared. "Have a good meeting, Morgan."

I stood, rubbing the back of my neck. They had such an interesting relationship.

"I'll see you on Sunday?" I asked.

Thomas glanced at me, finally cracking a smile. "Yeah."

"Good. I better run before I'm late."

"Don't do anything I wouldn't do," he said as he waved me away.

"Sounds like I want to do whatever James is doing," I replied, seeing the smile drop from his face.

When I turned around, James laughed, holding his stomach. "I can't believe you just said that."

"He was too damn serious." I wondered if Thomas was about to march out of the office and smack me upside the head. "So, where are you headed tonight?"

"Well," he said as we started to walk down the hallway, glancing over his shoulder, "it's a BDSM club."

My mouth fell open.

Oh my God. My little cousin was into that stuff?

"Like chains and whips?" I asked, trying to pick my jaw up off the floor.

James laughed harder, shaking his head as he slapped me on the back. "Something like that. It's more about dominance and submission."

"Izzy bosses you around a lot?"

"No, young man." James's face turned very serious. "I boss her around."

"But I thought..."

James grinned. "I'm the dominant in that relationship."

"Izzy is so bossy though." I gawked at him.

"She acts out all the time. I think she does it on purpose just so I'll punish her."

I swallowed hard, trying to wipe that mental image from my mind. "I don't want to know." I fully understood why Thomas didn't want to hear about it. "She's my little cousin, man."

"Not into it?" he asked as we walked into the reception area.

"I never said that. I just don't want to hear about you and Izzy there though."

"James, are you and Izzy going to the place that shall not be named?" Angel teased, standing from her desk and walking over to us with a playful smile.

"Yeah, Angel. Tonight's our night out."

"Lucky bitch." Angel laughed. "Mention that in front of Thomas?" She chewed her lip, peering down the hallway.

"I may have."

"Fuck," she said, shaking her head. "Now he's going to be all pissy."

James bent down and kissed her cheek. "I'm sure you can put a smile back on his face, darling."

"True." She practically skipped toward his office.

"If you ever want to go there, just let me know. I can introduce you to a bunch of people. I'm sure you'd be a big hit there," James offered.

"I don't know much about it." I couldn't say that my interest wasn't piqued.

"I can teach you the ropes."

"You know there's so much shit I can say with all the double meaning I'm getting from you." I shook my head.

"I know. Just think about it."

"I will." I pushed the front door open. "Catch ya Sunday, man."

"Have a good night," he said as he stood in the lobby, his chest inflated and his feet shoulder-width apart, a smug smirk on his face.

"Not as good as you, I'm sure," I replied as the door swung closed behind me.

If I went any longer without a little excitement, I might have to take James up on his offer.

Life was getting dull.

CHAPTER SEVEN

RACE

Clusterfuck

I stomped down the sidewalk to the Fly Bar, my high heels clicking against the cement, barely missing the divots in the shitty sidewalk. I swear to God, if I fell, I'd kick him in the balls for making me come to this dive.

I'm the one who hired him, not the other way around.

By the time I walked inside, my clothes were damp and my throat was so dry. I needed a gallon of water to quench my thirst.

I shook the thoughts of his balls out of my mind as I walked toward the bar. He was leaning back in his chair and sipping a drink, oblivious to my presence.

I cleared my throat as I approached. I needed to be tough or at least act like the pit bull I'd become known as. I couldn't show weakness.

Not to him or any other man or I'd be eaten alive.

I squared my shoulders, shifting slightly. "Mr. DeLuca."

"Race." He didn't turn around.

I took a moment and studied him. His shoulders looked broader than I had fantasized about this week.

The corded muscles of his neck looked more taut and strained where they connected. I wanted to touch him, feel the strength underneath his clothes.

I pushed my thoughts away before I sat down, tossing my purse on the bar. "I'm here as ordered."

"Good." He stared at the television screen. "Cubs are doing crappy this year," he mumbled as he tossed some peanuts in his mouth. His stubble was back, giving him the look I'd come to love. The tiny hairs dotting his face moved together as if in a choreographed dance as he chewed.

I wanted to reach out and run my fingers across them to see if they were as coarse as they looked. "I hate baseball," I muttered, looking around the bar, trying not to stare at him.

"Such a shame." He glanced at me. "You're flushed. Are you okay?" He tilted his head, studying me.

I peered at him out of the corner of my eye. "It's hotter than hell outside. I just walked two blocks in high heels from where I parked to get here. Naturally, I'm flushed." I fanned myself, playing off the attraction I could no longer deny.

"Well, let's get you a cold drink to help cool you off." He snapped his fingers and the bartender walked toward us quickly.

I shook my head, blowing out a breath.

All he had to do to get service was beckon her, but me—I had to wait to be noticed.

"Thanks," I mumbled through gritted teeth.

She leaned over the bar, showing off her tits as she rested her chin in her hand. "Can I get you another?"

"I'll take a martini, extra dirty," I snarled.

She glanced at me and turned her attention back to him. "And you, handsome?" She batted her eyelashes, ignoring me.

Seriously.

It took everything in me not to reach over the bar and crack her. Women like her were the reason I had the problems I did at work.

"He'll take another, sweetheart," I snapped, the vein in my temple pulsing.

"Just another beer, Lisa."

She nodded, glaring at me as she began to walk away.

Fuck, he was on a first-name basis with her.

Does he like her?

"She's probably going to spit in my drink."

"You'd kind of deserve it if she does."

I looked at him, trying to remain calm. "I didn't need to see her tits hanging out. I just wanted to order a drink and speak with the man I hired about my case. We're here for work, not tits."

He stared at me, not saying a word as Lisa set our drinks down.

I ignored Lisa as she lingered a little too long. "This is a business meeting." I kept my gaze locked on his, wringing my hands together in my lap.

"I know, but you don't have to be so uptight. It's Friday, we're at a bar, and I'm in good company. Unwind a little. We have a lot to talk about," he said. Then his tongue darted out and swept across his lips.

My eyes dropped to his mouth. My skin flushed as his tongue swept across his lip. I fisted my fingers and kept them in my lap.

When his tongue disappeared, a grin spread across his face. "Can we drink to that?" he asked.

My eyes shot up to his. "To what?"

"Unwinding and good company?" He smirked, holding his glass up and covering his lips with the liquid.

"I'll drink to something cold and a tit-free zone." My eyes wandered down his arm to his biceps. I swallowed hard, noticing the way the T-shirt cut into his flesh.

"Fine." He chuckled. "To titless women and cold company."

I raised my glass, not realizing exactly what he'd said, and swallowed a mouthful.

As I set my glass down, I averted my eyes. "So, what news do you have to share with me?" I asked as I tapped the olive-laden toothpick against the rim of the glass.

He explained every procedure and boring fact he'd uncovered. At some point, I think I zoned out, because the next thing I knew, a new drink appeared in front of me.

Without interrupting him, I sipped my drink and listened to him babble on about tech bullshit. I let him go on and on and stared at his lips as they moved with each word. By the time I'd nearly finished the second drink, he was ready to give me the information I'd been waiting to hear.

"I tracked the IP address from your e-mail and used other methods to find the culprit. I was shocked to find that the IP originated not in New York, but from right here in Tampa."

I recoiled, my mouth falling open. "Tampa?"

He nodded, turning the beer in his hands. "Yeah. I was surprised. I thought, based on the information you gave me, that it would be from New York too. It doesn't mean that it couldn't be someone on the list you gave me, but we need to expand our search parameters."

"Fuck," I mumbled. "This is a complete clusterfuck." I bit my lip.

"I'll get it solved, Race. Don't ever fear that." He gave me a sweet smile. "Who here would want to harm your reputation?"

I winced as I shook my head. "The question is who doesn't."

His face fell. "Are you that unlikeable?"

"I work in a male-dominated industry. I'm not the type of girl to take shit from anyone," I said as I rubbed my face, barely having any feeling in my cheeks. "I've made a lot of enemies at work. No one likes a woman executive, especially the men who think they're better than I am."

"Is it really that brutal?"

"More brutal than you could ever imagine, Morgan," I said.

He stroked his lip. "Let's start with your competition at work first. Anyone who would be threatened by your success?"

I swirled the last of the liquid in my glass, trying to avoid looking at him. "I could fill a notebook." I started to feel sorry for myself. "I think I need another." I tipped my glass, noticing that it was basically empty.

God, I had so many haters.

Was it because I was a bitch? I hated the term. I thought I was tough, but I heard the murmurs in the office and the whispers about being the biggest bitch in the company when I walked by.

I never put much thought into people liking me. I didn't give a shit if I made friends, either. The only thing I cared about was being successful and doing a good job. Now, I had to watch my back and wonder about who wished for my failure enough to threaten me.

"Write down their names." He pushed the paper in front of me.

I jotted down twenty names, mostly males, of people I could picture wanting to see me crash and burn.

"Do you have any friends, with a list of enemies that long?" he asked, pushing the drink closer to me.

I dropped the pen and clasped my hands together. "Not really."

"Too busy trying to get ahead?"

For some reason, his statement made me giggle. "Yeah, something like that." I giggled again as I glanced at him.

He wrinkled his nose. "Maybe I should cut you off." He put his hand over the glass and started to pull it toward him.

I scowled and moved quickly, placing my hand over his. "Don't you dare. I need that drink. I earned that drink this week, goddammit."

"Whatever you say," he whispered.

The warmth of his hands had my thoughts drifting to the feel of them caressing my breasts. My face flushed as I realized he was staring at me.

"You feeling okay, Race?" The corner of his mouth twitched.

I cleared my throat. "Just a little warm from the weather still. I can't seem to cool off." I fanned myself, pulling on the collar of my blouse.

"Sure." He grinned, pulling his hand from my drink. "You want ice water instead? Maybe that would help cool you off." He raised an eyebrow.

"Nope, just another martini." I brought the glass to my mouth, watching Morgan over the rim as I polished it off.

I needed to get myself together.

I didn't have time to fantasize.

There was someone after me, and I needed to focus on that. One slipup and whoever had it in for me would probably pounce on my shit and use it as an opportunity to ruin me.

I made a mental note—all future conversations were to take place over the telephone.

One-on-one contact could be hazardous to my health.

CHAPTER EIGHT

MORGAN

Martini Madness

"You're really purdy," she slurred with a lopsided grin, running her finger down my cheek.

"That's it. No more drinks for you." I dragged the glass away from her.

"No! I've only had three." She lurched forward, pulling the drink out of my hands. "I'm enjoying myself. I've had a bitch of a week and I deserve to let loose a little."

I held my hands up. "You've actually had four martinis, but anything you want, princess."

Her eyes grew into little slits. "I'm not your princess."

My cheeks hurt as I smiled. "I'm going to take you home now. I think you need to sleep it off."

"Last time I checked," she said before hiccupping, "you're not my daddy." A slow smile crept across her face. She scooted closer and whispered, "Unless that's your thing." She tried to wink, but both eyes closed, one after the other.

I leaned into her space, a breath away from her lips. "It's not my thing, but I'm happy to act out your fantasies. But I don't think you want to cross that line. Once you go there, there's no going back." I stared into her eyes.

"Oooh." Her eyes grew wide. "Is that supposed to scare me, Mr. DeLuca?"

I didn't move. "I'm just giving you fair warning. You've had a few drinks, and I won't take advantage of that. I'm just telling you how it is."

"You're full of yourself." Her warm, sweet breath caressed my lips as she spoke.

All I wanted to do was reach out, pull her face to mine, and kiss her full, beautiful lips. "I'm sure of myself and confident in my abilities, yes. That's entirely different than being full of myself." I licked my lips, testing her.

Her eyes dropped to my mouth as her lips parted.

"Another?" Lisa interrupted.

"We're good." I kept my eyes pinned to Race and waving Lisa off.

"Pfft," Lisa scoffed, stomping away.

Race glared in Lisa's direction. "She wants you."

Was she jealous?

"I don't want her."

"She's a sure thing though."

I leaned closer, leaving very little space between us. "I never liked easy."

"All men like easy." Her body swayed, moving so close our lips almost brushed.

Yep, she was definitely jealous.

I reached out, steadying her. "Maybe for a cheap fuck, but nothing more."

Her body jolted as someone bumped into her chair and she tumbled forward, her face landing against my chest.

"Watch it, asshole," I barked.

"Fuck off," the drunk asshole called out as he staggered away.

"Don't," she muttered into my chest, her hands squeezing my thighs.

I grabbed her arms, starting to stand.

"No," she yelled into my chest, trying to hold me in place. "Don't start a fight."

I grunted, staying in my chair. I didn't want the night to end already. I couldn't risk Race getting upset with me.

I grabbed her shoulders and tried to prop her upright.

"Gimme a minute," she said, her voice muffled by my shirt.

"He should apologize to you," I growled, trying to find him in the sea of people.

Her fingertips dug into my skin as she felt my thighs. She nestled her face deeper into my chest, her warm breath coming through my shirt.

"Come on, big girl. Let's get you home." I lifted her, pushing her against the chair.

"I'm not ready to go home though," she whined as her eyes tried to focus on me but crossed instead.

"I think it's best for us both if I take you home."

"I'll grab a cab." She straightened and started to tip sideways.

I shook my head and held her up with one hand. "I'd feel better if I took you home."

"I'd feel better with you in my home too." She leaned into my touch.

"Okay, Race. That's it." I stood, reached in my pocket for a fifty, and tossed it on the bar. "Come on, lightweight. Let's get you to bed."

"Mmm." She tried to stand. "Bed sounds perfect."

I held her by the waist as she stumbled out of the restaurant on unsteady feet. When we hit the sidewalk, I lifted her into my arms.

"Oh my God," she screeched, batting at my chest. "Put me down."

I held her tight as she started to wiggle. "You can't walk in those heels on this shitty, cracked sidewalk. You'll fall and break your neck. Stop wigglin', woman, or I'll drop you," I lied.

She weighed nothing, but I'd use it as an excuse to hold her for a little while. Relaxing, she laid her head on my shoulder.

"Are you smelling me?" she asked as we approached my car.

"No." I moved my face away from her head, knowing I'd been caught. I couldn't get enough of her sweet scent.

"Surrre." She snuggled into me.

"We're here." I looked down at her and smiled.

"I'm so tired," she mumbled, sagging closer to me, "and comfortable."

"I'm going to put you down now," I warned her before releasing my grip.

She slid down my body, letting her face press against my chest. I didn't bother to hide my amusement. I pushed her back and propped her against the car as I unlocked it and opened the door. "In ya go." I held her by the arm, making sure she got in without banging her head.

"You're really a nice guy," she said, blinking slowly, out of sync, as her body swayed.

"Let's keep that our little secret." I lifted her legs inside and closed the door. "Lord give me strength not to fuck this up." I glanced upward as I walked around the car. "I cannot sleep with her."

The hard dick inside my pants begged to differ, but I knew I couldn't take advantage of her. That was what I'd be doing if I let tonight get out of control.

I can't fuck her tonight.

CHAPTER NINE

RACE

It's Now or Never

"**M**organ," I whispered as he carried me inside my house.

"Yeah?" he asked, staring down at me.

"I'm not that drunk," I whispered.

"But you are, princess." He opened my bedroom door and carried me inside.

"I'm not," I argued, sliding my hand up his neck and holding his cheek, slowly stroking the fresh stubble.

"What are you doing?" His fingers dug into my hip.

"I want you." I brushed my lips across his chin.

"We shouldn't, Race," he told me.

"I don't care what we should do. Don't you want me?" I murmured against his skin.

He closed his eyes, inhaling deeply. "I do, but you're going to regret it in the morning," he said, giving me another chance to back out.

There was no way in hell I'd say no.

I wanted Morgan DeLuca.

After a week of fantasizing about nothing but him, I had my chance to make it a reality.

"I wanted you the moment I saw that big guy standing in the doorway, looking like he was ready to kick someone's ass. I wanted to grab your muscles"—I held his forearm, squeezing it gently—"taste your skin, and feel you inside me."

"I wanted you before I knew your name." He laid me down on the bed.

I looped my arms around his neck, bringing his face closer. "Kiss me, then," I murmured, moving my mouth toward his.

Hell yes.

His nostrils flared as his breath grew harsh. He crushed his lips to mine, breathing me in as he kissed me. His mouth was softer than I'd fantasized, with the perfect amount of tongue and lip.

I moaned into his mouth, feeling my body tingle all over. It was so cliché, but it happened.

I ran my fingers through his hair, dragging my nails against his scalp. He shuddered, moaning and driving forward into my mouth. His tongue swept inside, tasting me as I wrapped my legs around his back, holding him against my body.

He was hard. Rock hard. As he pressed against me, I ground my pussy against his length, loving the friction as our bodies rubbed together.

"Don't," he murmured into my mouth.

I smiled against his lips. "Why?"

"I want you so badly. I don't want this to be over before it starts," he growled.

I groaned, pretending to be sad, but his words made me wet. Morgan DeLuca was kissing me. He was in my bed, on top of me, and he wanted me. I unhooked my legs from his body, instantly missing the contact.

His hand slid down my body, finding my breast. As his finger swept across my hardened nipple, I felt the air leave my body. He inhaled it, bringing it into him.

"Morgan," I moaned with the last ounce of breath I had.

He grunted as his hand skated across my torso and found the edge of my shirt, slipping underneath. Tiny sparks skidded across my skin as his hand swept over my stomach on a collision course with my breasts.

My belly flipped when his finger stroked the edge of my bra. The warmth of his palm didn't stop the goose bumps that erupted across my skin.

When the front closure to my bra popped, my breasts sprang free.

"Mm." He cupped my breast, sweeping a thumb across my nipple. "So fucking soft."

As his hand vanished, I whimpered, missing the contact. Had he changed his mind? My eyes popped open as his lips left mine. My body stiffened as my stomach flipped and he sat back, resting his body on his heels.

He stared down at me with a sly grin. "Sit up," he whispered. "I need you naked."

Relief flooded my body. The butterflies that had been floating around my insides transformed. I sat up and started to lift my shirt.

He placed his hands over mine, stopping me. "No." He peered down at me. "I want to undress you."

My damn system went into overdrive. Morgan DeLuca wanted to undress me. He wanted to fuck me. If I'd been sober, I might have thought about the repercussions, but the alcohol helped me relax enough to share my true feelings.

I could no longer deny that I wanted him. I couldn't deny him any longer. I had hoped for a kiss when the night ended, but I was getting so much more.

I lifted my arms, glancing up at him as my shirt and bra were quickly removed and tossed to the floor. If I'd been sober, I might have covered myself up. Between the liquor and the burning in his eyes, I did the opposite. I soaked in the way he was looking at me as he slid my skirt down my legs.

"Morgan," I blurted out, feeling a bit self-conscious, but not about my body.

"Yeah?" he asked as he threw my panties and skirt in the same place as my top. As he crawled off the bed and removed his shirt, I couldn't help but stare.

His chest looked harder and bigger than it had underneath the formfitting T-shirts he wore. My eyes raked over every ripple of his six-pack and I felt my mouth water as he unzipped his jeans.

I knew I wasn't going to be disappointed, but seeing it and feeling it were entirely different. I'd felt him between my legs, hard and big. But it had been so long since I'd had sex, and I wanted Morgan so much that I wondered if it was a mirage. When his dick sprang free, I was secretly scared.

There's such a thing as too big. Especially when I hadn't fucked anyone in a year. I read somewhere that a pussy snaps back to virginal tightness after being empty for so long. I wouldn't be shocked if mine was sealed closed with cobwebs inside.

As I swallowed hard, he crawled onto the bed and settled between my legs, pressing his eight inches of hardness against me.

"I want to warn you," I said with a raspy voice.

He shook his head, leaning forward and placing his finger over my lips. "I don't want to know. Stop thinking so much."

"But I..." I mumbled against his fingers, staring up at him.

"Let it go. It doesn't matter." He placed a hand against my belly, coaxing me flat against the mattress. "All that matters is I want to bury myself so deep inside you that everything else disappears."

All thoughts vanished as his lips found my neck. When his teeth sank into my shoulder, I shivered. That was my spot. The special one that made my entire body burst into flames.

As his mouth carved a path of ecstasy down my torso, I closed my eyes and enjoyed the feel of him on me. His mouth sizzled as he stroked my nipple with his tongue, and I opened my legs wider, needing more.

"So fucking beautiful," he muttered against the skin right above my pubic hair.

The tiny hairs swayed as his breath drifted down. Each one moved, sending a tingle down my legs. I could feel the wetness between my legs. I didn't think I'd ever been so turned on in my life.

When he placed his mouth against my pussy, kissing me more fiercely than he had my mouth, I almost exploded. My body arched as the ache between my legs grew more intense.

"Morgan." My eyes rolled back in my head.

He mumbled against my clit and my body trembled in response. As he slipped a single, thick digit inside me, I fisted the sheets.

"Oh God." I relished the fullness I felt and moaned again.

He stroked my insides as his mouth caressed my skin. I needed to come so badly, but just as it was about to break free, he stopped. I lifted my head and stared at him, ready to scream.

"Not yet," he said. "Don't tense."

I tossed my head back against the pillow, and tried to relax. He slipped his fingers out as his mouth found me again. As he rubbed two fingers against my opening, I braced myself for impact, waiting for the familiar stretch I knew was coming from my unused body.

Inch by inch, he drove them forward, stretching me. To my surprise, I relished in the feel of the fullness. After a few more sweeps of his tongue against my clit, my body grew taut.

When his fingers curled inside me, rubbing my G-spot, I couldn't hold it together. I exploded. The orgasm ripped through my body as my pussy clamped down against his fingers. I couldn't breathe as the room spun. I never wanted the feeling to end.

I couldn't yell out or moan. I lay here stiff as my body rode out the wave of ecstasy crashing over me. As my body relaxed, I basked in the pleasure, and then he slipped his fingers out. Instantly, my core felt abandoned but deliciously used by him.

As he climbed up me, I sucked in air, trying to catch the tiny breaths I'd missed during the throes of passion.

"You got a condom?" He brushed his lips against mine.

Only me.

The condoms I had were older than the sour milk I had in the fridge. "No." I tasted myself on his mouth.

"I'm clean, Race. I was just tested and I haven't been with anyone since." He looked down on me with soft eyes.

I'd been on the pill to help control my cramps, so I wasn't worried about pregnancy. At my last checkup I got a clean bill of health, and I hadn't been with anyone besides my vibrator. I knew I was clean. "I'm clean too, and I'm on the pill," I announced, feeling his hard length settling between my legs.

"Is this okay? Do you trust me?" He rubbed the tip of his cock against my wetness.

In my infinite wisdom to get drunk and fuck Morgan DeLuca, I hadn't thought about protection. I'd assumed he was the type of guy who carried one around in his wallet, ready for action at a moment's notice.

Did I trust Morgan enough to let him fuck me without protection? Staring up into his eyes, I believed every word he'd whispered. I did trust him. I trusted him with my life and my body.

"I do," I whispered, swallowing down the lump that started to work its way down my throat.

Without another word, his cock poked my opening, and he drove the tip inside. The delicious ache returned, and I felt my body stretch to accommodate him. Every worry fell away, replaced by the need to feel him in my body.

When he shoved his dick inside me, I started to cry out as his mouth collided with mine and stole my breath once again.

His pelvis reared back and slammed into me. My back arched, driving him deeper as I stared, completely in awe.

Seeing each of his abdominal muscles ripple made my fingertips ache to touch them. I slid my hands down his back, finding the edge of the muscles and feeling them move underneath my fingers.

I stilled as he tugged on my legs, sat up slightly, and grabbed my ankles. I watched with wide eyes as he pulled them to the sides, creating a giant V.

His cock slammed, nothing stopping him from seating himself inside me fully. I closed my eyes, unable to watch as he stroked my insides.

"Open your eyes," he commanded in a stern but soft voice. "Look at me as I fuck you."

Without hesitation, I opened my eyes and watched him fuck me. Pleasure and lust burned in his eyes as he stared down at me and worked his cock in and out of my body. His lower body swayed as his shoulders remained still, and he gyrated his hips in the most delicious way.

"Touch yourself. I want to see you make yourself come as I fuck you."

I'd never touched myself in front of someone else, but with the way he was looking at me, I didn't hesitate. After sliding my hand down my midsection, I found my clit and began to caress around it.

The slickness from his mouth still lingered, making my fingers slide easily against my flesh. Every time he drove his cock inside, I moaned, moving my fingers closer to my clit.

Unable to resist, I circled my clit, letting the strokes grow harsher with each pass. I wanted this orgasm more than I'd needed the one he'd already given me. With the way his cock swept inside me, I couldn't wait any longer.

"That's it, baby. Come on my cock."

No one had ever dirty-talked me in bed before, and I suddenly realized its appeal.

I closed my eyes, concentrating on my strokes.

"Look at me when you come," he growled softly.

My eyes flew open as my finger brushed against my clit more deliberately. As he snaked his hips and I stroked between my legs, a burst of pleasure zipped throughout my body.

My toes curled; my head lifted from the pillow as my fingers faltered. The orgasm ripping through my system was greater than every previous orgasm I'd had in my life combined.

I tried to breathe, but I couldn't. My body locked, lungs and all, as the crest crashed down, pulling the life out of me. Morgan moaned, following me over the cliff and shuddering.

I clenched down, pulling him deeper as the aftershocks racked his body, matching my own.

We gasped for air, growing limp as he crushed his body against mine. My legs were stiff, aching from the unfamiliar position as they flopped on the bed. My body was spent, my mind hazy as I tried to bring the oxygen into my system.

When he rolled onto his side and pulled me against him, I went willingly. I nestled against him, sated, and drifted off to sleep with nothing on my mind but him.

CHAPTER TEN

MORGAN

I'm So Fucked

I slept with my client.
No. I fucked Race True.

The memory of last night came back to me as I opened my eyes. The way she had called out my name, the sound of her moans, and the massive orgasm that had ripped through me made me smile.

Race True was more than I'd bargained for. I'd known the moment I saw her that I wanted her.

She stirred, pulling the comforter against her chest.

Sitting up, I watched her as soft snores fell from her lips.

There was so much about the woman I didn't know. The one thing I knew for sure was that I wanted to know everything about her.

Last night wasn't the end.

It couldn't be.

I'd been with plenty of women in my life, but no one like her.

I'm so fucked.
I slept with my client.

If she woke up and regretted last night, she could have me fired. Thomas would probably murder me if he found out. Anxiety gripped me.

"Morning," she whispered, stretching her arms.

"Morning, beautiful." I felt instantly relieved.

"I slept like a rock." She kicked the covers back, contorting her body like I'd never seen as she yawned.

"Me too."

Last night, I'd passed out cold, holding her body and twirling my fingers in her hair.

"Come here, Race." I patted my leg, wanting to touch her.

"You want me to suck your dick already?" Her eyes widened.

"If you're offering." I laughed. "I just want to talk."

"Oh," she mumbled before setting her head on my thigh.

I dug my fingers into her hair, stroking the yellow silk. "I want to talk about last night."

She rolled over and peered up at me. "What's to talk about?"

"Are you okay?" I swallowed hard, stilling my hands in her hair. "I mean, are we okay?"

"Do you think I regret it? Or that I was too drunk to know what I was doing?"

I bit my lip and took a deep breath. "Yeah."

"Morgan," she whispered, rubbing her cheek against my thigh, "I don't regret a minute of last night."

"Phew." I started to stroke her hair again, loving the way it fell through my fingertips. "Because it was fan-fucking-tastic."

She giggled, nodding her head. "It was, and I told you I wasn't drunk," she said, relaxing against me.

"You were pretty drunk."

"By the time we got back here, I'd sobered enough to know what I was asking for. I don't regret a minute of it."

I closed my eyes, resting my head against the headboard. "You shouldn't. I was pretty spectacular." I peeked at her with one eye.

"You're an asshole." She slapped my stomach. "Morgan," she whispered, tracing the contours of my abdomen with her fingers where her hand had just swatted.

"Yeah?" I asked, getting lost in the pattern.

"Do you think we should stop working together? I mean, can you still work on my case after what we did?" Her finger stilled, remaining flush against my skin.

I didn't answer right away as I thought about it. "Yeah, Race. I want to finish your case. There's nothing more that I want than for you to be safe." I knew that no one else would work as hard for her. "No one has more to gain by the case being over than I do."

She lifted herself, glancing up at me as the creases in her forehead deepened. "What do you have to gain, Mr. DeLuca?"

"You, Ms. True," I said matter-of-factly. "I have everything to lose if I don't get it right and more than I deserve if I solve your case."

"How do you know I didn't just want to sleep with you and be done?" She smirked.

"Come on, princess. I saw how you looked at me when you came with my dick buried inside you."

"Sweetie, that was lust."

I shook my head, pursing my lips. "That was more than lust."

"I like you, Morgan, but let's not go overboard." She laid her head back down. "Although, I'll admit, I do love your cock."

"It's a start," I lied, because although she couldn't say the words, her body betrayed her. "You can lie to yourself all you want, but I know the truth." I winked at her.

"I have to go into the office," she muttered, closing her eyes.

"It's Saturday."

"So? Are you going to work today?" She stroked the V on my abdomen.

"Yeah. After I find a place to live."

"See. We're both workaholics," she teased, raking her fingernails across my skin.

"Only because I want to solve your case."

"Good answer."

I glanced at the clock, realizing I had an hour. "I have to go, but I don't feel like moving."

"Mmm," she mumbled.

"I have an appointment with my realtor."

She sat up. "You better go, then." She let the sheets fall from her body as she smirked.

I stared at her chest as my morning boner grew larger, ready to break off. "I have a little time." I leaned forward. "Do you?" I murmured against her skin.

"I can make time."

"I see that look in your eye," I told her, sweeping my tongue across her neck.

"Morgan," she whispered, her voice breathy, "just fuck me and shut up."

I bit down on her neck. "I like a woman who knows what she wants."

"Shh." She palmed my dick. "Less talking."

I fucked Race one more time before I left. I didn't know if it would be the last time I'd have her. I memorized every angle, storing it away for later.

I walked outside on unsteady legs, perfectly spent.

Things had shifted between us, and my life seemed to be falling into place.

Maybe I was reading more into it than I should've been. But there's a look I know, one that conveys every emotion that's left unspoken. I saw it in her eyes.

She wanted to know me as much as I wanted to find out who the real Race True was, and it made me happy.

I walked down the driveway and climbed in my car, savoring the memory of her calling my name.

Life was good.

CHAPTER ELEVEN

RACE

How Did That Happen?

Oh my God. *I slept Morgan DeLuca.*

Actually, he'd fucked me, and I wasn't ashamed to admit that I'd loved every minute of it.

He'd cuddled me too. Held me in his arms all night, and I fucking loved it.

"What's that grin about?" Cara asked as she walked into my office.

"Oh, nothing." I rocked back and forth in my chair.

"I've worked for you long enough to know you." She cocked an eyebrow as she started to tidy my desk.

Cara had been assigned to me my first day on the job. As I'd climbed the ranks, she'd come with me and remained forever loyal. I didn't think it could be possible to have a better secretary than her. More importantly, she was my best friend, and I always confided in her.

She glanced at me. "It's that man, isn't it?"

"Who?" My voice squeaked.

"You've had two meetings now with that man from the investigation company."

"He's nice." I fidgeted with my pen.

"Sure. Why are you so red now that I've mentioned him?" She tilted her head, smirking.

"It's hot in here."

"It's not. So, you like him?" she asked. "Have you kissed him?"

"Cara." I tried not to smile.

She shook her head and giggled. "It doesn't matter. Whatever he's done, I like seeing you happy."

"Yeah." I couldn't look her in the eye.

"Don't forget what today is." She grabbed a stack of folders from the outgoing bin on the bureau.

"I know." A knot formed in my stomach.

"Did you want me to grab some flowers for you?" she asked, stopping at the door.

"No. I'll do it." I shook my head. "Why don't you leave early today? There's no reason for you to work on the weekends with me, Cara."

"I like spending time with you, Race. You know that. My kids are grown, my husband passed, and I can't just sit at home all day. I'd go crazy."

"Well, I love having you around, Cara. You're more than just my secretary."

"I know, kid. I know. I think you should take the day off too." She held the door open as she balanced the stack of files in her arms.

I glanced over my desk, realizing I didn't have anything else to do. "I'll head out soon."

"See you Monday," she said before leaving.

"Monday," I repeated, grabbing my purse and following her into the lobby.

Today was the anniversary of my father's death.

Where did fifteen years go?

Even though time had passed, the soul-crushing sadness of losing my dad hadn't diminished. Every day I thought about him. There were times when I missed him more than others, but there wasn't a moment that passed that I didn't long to be in his arms.

Tears fell from my eyes, plopping on the grass as I stood in front of his grave. "Daddy," I whispered as I collapsed into the grass. "I'm so sorry," I wailed, covering my face. "I should've come sooner."

As each year passed, I came to visit less and less. The guilt I experienced when I came sucked the life out of me. I couldn't spend my weekends here, feeling the weight of his death on my shoulders.

He had been my entire world, and the only one in my family who had shown me unconditional love. He'd brought me everywhere with him, much to my mother's dismay. We'd secretly snuck to the racetrack on weekends, enjoying our time out of the city together.

My dad had been my best friend. There was nothing I'd loved more than being his little girl. When he died, a piece of me was buried with him.

My mother grew more hateful with each passing day. By the time I'd gone to college, we'd stopped speaking. Really, I'd stopped talking to her because I couldn't take her bullshit anymore. Somehow she'd come to the conclusion that it was my fault my father had died.

He died instantly one day after work when he'd come to pick me up from school. She'd said that his need to make me happy by not requiring me to take the school bus was the cause. Not the semi that had plowed through the back of his SUV, but me. In her mind, I was the one who killed him.

After placing the flowers on his grave, I pushed myself up and kissed his headstone. "I love you, Daddy," I whispered, another wave of sobs breaking free.

I would've given anything to hear him call my name again.

I knew loss.

It was part of me.

My father was my first love—and the first one to leave me behind.

Everyone left me.

I couldn't let myself feel anything for Morgan. I didn't think I could take another heartbreak without losing myself completely in the blackness.

CHAPTER TWELVE

MORGAN

Family Dinner

"How's work going?" Uncle Sal asked.

"Good. Good."

"He's been a huge help, Pop." Thomas gave me a brief nod. "We really needed him. Hell, we still could use a few guys to help pick up the slack."

"It's always good to be in demand, son."

I should've felt guilty about Friday night, but I didn't. I didn't regret a moment I'd spent with Race.

"Yeah. James and I are throwing around a couple names of people we could recruit to join us." Thomas put his feet up on the coffee table.

"Anyone I know?" Uncle Sal raised an eyebrow.

"You do, but I don't want to talk about work today. I'm still trying to convince James that he's the right man for the job."

"Sam?"

James mashed his hands together and gritted his teeth. "You know I hate him."

Thomas looked over at James and grinned. "We've already been over this."

"Have you talked to your mom today, Morgan?" Auntie Mar walked into the living room.

"Not today. Something happen?" My heart began to beat erratically.

"She said she'd be here by next weekend." She smiled as she sat on the arm of the couch.

"Great," I said in a quiet voice through closed teeth.

"You're a horrible liar." Auntie Mar hit me with the kitchen towel.

"I love her, but the woman is so overbearing sometimes."

"We're mothers. We're supposed to be."

That was always the excuse my mother gave me. It was their job to be annoying and nosy as hell.

"But it would be nice if she could let go just a little."

Aunt Mar laughed. "Never going to happen," she said before she stood and headed back to the kitchen.

Joe nudged me with his elbow. "You just have to learn how to handle them."

"Yep," Mike agreed from the chair in the corner, nodding slowly.

"Pretend like you're listening and learn to ignore her. That's what I do with Ma." Anthony pulled his wife, Max, into his lap.

"I can hear you," Auntie Mar yelled from the kitchen.

"Ma isn't that bad," Thomas added.

All eyes turned to him.

"That's because you were gone so long. If it weren't for that, you'd get the same bullshit we all do." Joe's eyes darted toward the kitchen.

"Oh, please. She just loves us." Thomas puffed his chest out.

"Lies. All lies." Izzy slid between James's legs on the floor.

I felt envious of the Gallos.

They had each other.

I'd been alone my entire life, with no brothers or sister to tease or have my back. I missed my ma, but I'd never admit it. And if I was being entirely truthful, I wished Race were here with me.

"What's wrong?" Joe asked.

I blinked a couple of times and focused on him. "Me?" I scrunched my nose.

"Yeah, you."

"Nothing, man."

"Something's on your mind, cousin. Spit it out," Joe said, running his finger across his lip.

I scrubbed my hands across my face. "Just thinking about how lucky you are to have each other."

"Dude, it must've sucked being an only child," Mike chimed in, shaking his head as he winced.

I shrugged. "At times, it was great. I didn't have to share shit with anyone, but then at other times..."

"Yeah. It has to be lonely," Mike said.

"I call bullshit. I'd love to be an only child," Izzy blurted out. "I'd want all the attention. Plus, I wouldn't have had to put up with your asses my entire life."

"Izzy." Anthony gave her a nasty look, "Please stop with your crap. You've been treated like an only child for years. You're a girl, and that's afforded you a pretty charmed existence."

"That's such a crock of crap." She rolled her eyes.

In the other room, the older kids played in the new playroom Auntie Mar had made for them. The Gallos were creating a small army. Izzy had twin boys about six months before her wedding and named them Rocco and Carmello, but everyone called him Mello. Thomas and Angel had a little boy, Nick, who was just learning to walk. Anthony, Joe, and Mike each had little girls named Tamara, Gigi, and Lily respectively.

"I better go get Nick up so he's ready to eat, baby," Angel said to Thomas before kissing him on the cheek and heading upstairs.

"James." Izzy glanced at him.

"What?"

"I need help carrying those two beasts you helped create." Izzy stood and put her hands on her hips.

"I got ya. I'll get them both, love. You rest." He pulled her back down onto the floor and nuzzled his face into her neck. "I love waking the boys up," he mumbled against her skin.

"Nah. I want to help you." She giggled as she climbed to her feet and pulled James with her.

The living room thinned quickly. I took it as a cue to go see if Auntie Mar needed any help. The least I could do was pitch in, since she had been gracious enough to invite me.

"Hey, Auntie Mar." I walked into the kitchen, finding her spooning the meatballs into a giant bowl. "Let me help you."

"You're such a dear, Morgan." She turned and gave me a magnificent smile. "Can you finish this while I get the gnocchi ready?"

"Hell yeah." Gnocchi was my favorite. The shit sat in my stomach like a ton of bricks, but it was amazingly soft.

She handed me the spoon. "You're really a good man. You've changed so much since you were a teenager."

"I hope so. I was a punk back then."

"We all have to grow up sometime. You just took the harder road." She bent over and pulled a strainer that could fit at least three pounds of pasta in it without a problem out of the cupboard.

"Joining the army was the best thing for me. My mom would disagree, but I don't know if I'd be alive today if it weren't for them."

She placed the strainer in the sink and turned toward me. "Morgan." She placed her hand on my shoulder. "Your mom knows it was the best thing for you. She just likes to complain. Plus," she added as she turned her attention back to the pasta, "it's the job of a mother to make her children feel guilty." She was surrounded by a cloud of steam as she dumped the boiling water and pasta into the sink.

I dropped the last meatball in the bowl and watched as she shook the water out of the pasta. "You're all crazy."

"We'd be boring if we weren't. Be a dear and go set those meatballs on the dining room table. We're just about done here."

"Yes, ma'am." I saluted her.

"Smartass. You're all the same."

"Touché, Aunt Mar." I wished I had used a potholder to carry the damn bowl.

For the first time in forever, I felt like I had a family again. I belonged somewhere. Although they were my cousins, I loved them like we were more. We'd spent our youth together, tearing shit up and causing trouble in the neighborhood.

That was until Joe and I had gotten into just enough trouble to make Auntie Mar and Uncle Sal pack the kids up and leave town. It was the worst feeling ever.

I stared around the dining room table, looking at each of the chairs, and said to myself, "I'm a lucky son of a bitch." I left out the bit about Race.

Just then, Aunt Mar yelled, "Dinner!" as she carried the gnocchi into the dining room with the potholders I'd decided not to use.

"Thanks," I said as I turned to her.

"For what?" She set the bowl on the table.

"For being my family." I gave her a kiss on the cheek.

"Who knew you were such a softy, Morgan?"

"This doesn't go any further. Got me?"

"Too late," Joe said as he walked in the room. "I'm going to buy your ass a purse to carry around all those feelings in."

"Don't you start, Joseph," Aunt Mar warned him. "You aren't as tough as you look, son. People in glass houses—"

"Yeah, yeah," he interrupted. "I got ya."

"What did I miss?" Izzy asked as she walked in behind Suzy, carrying Mello. Or maybe it was Rocco. I couldn't tell them apart yet.

"Nothing, Izzy. Let's eat." Joe pulled the chair out for his wife.

One by one, everyone entered the dining room, taking their spots at the table. Even I had my own chair. I was a full-fledged member of the family.

This time, I wouldn't do anything to fuck it up.

CHAPTER THIRTEEN

RACE

I'm Totally Fucked

I hated Sundays.

They were useless.

I'd always planned to spend my Sundays on the beach, sipping wine, and reading a good book, but it never happened. Typically, I sat home, did laundry, and worked in my pajamas.

I hadn't been able to get Morgan off my mind. I knew I shouldn't want to be with him, but I wanted it more than anything in the world. I wouldn't survive him. I knew that.

When I checked my e-mail before settling down to watch a movie, what popped up on my screen rattled me.

> **Race,**
> **He can't help you. No one can. You're in my crosshairs and I'm coming for you when you least expect it.**

My heart started to pound as I glanced around, wondering if someone was outside my house. I grabbed my phone and texted Morgan.

Morgan: I'll be right over. Stay put.
Me: No. I'm fine. I just wanted to make you aware.

I unlocked and relocked my French doors to the back deck as I waited for his reply, and then I peeked through the blinds, trying to see if someone was outside.

Morgan: I'm coming over, Race. I need to do a perimeter check. I'll bring the others to help and stay with you for a while. No lip.

I didn't expect him to rush right over. I felt guilty for pulling him away from whatever he was doing tonight.

Me: No. There's no one here. I'm fine. Really.
Morgan: Stay inside, lock the doors, and stay away from the windows. I'll be there in twenty.

Duh! I mean, seriously. Did he think I was going to stand outside and sing a song?

Me: Yes, sir.

I turned the lights off and tried to distract myself while I waited.

I settled on the couch, watching *The Bachelor* and the train wreck that happened every episode. It was always good for a laugh. I started to drift off during the rose ceremony, my eyes feeling heavy and starting to sting.

My doorbell rang and I jumped.

"Race!" Morgan yelled as he knocked on the door. "Race, answer the goddamn door."

"Coming." I stomped toward the door. I checked my reflection in the mirror. My eyes were red, with bags underneath. Great. My pajamas were okay, but they were nothing he hadn't seen before. Really, it was just a pair of shorts and a tank top. I wasn't about to make it look like I'd made an effort.

This was business, I reminded myself as I reached for the door, not sex.

"Race. I'm going to bust this door down if you don't open it." He pounded on the door this time.

The man was such a spaz. "What the hell?" I threw my hands up after I opened the door.

His eyes were on fire as he breathed hard. "What the hell? That's all you have to say?" His hands rested on the frame with two men behind him.

"Well, yeah. I mean, I'm fine, and there's no reason to threaten to bust down my door. I yelled 'Coming.'"

"I wouldn't let a door stand between me and your safety." He gave me a halfhearted smile.

"I'm fine. I haven't been murdered." I opened the door wide enough to let them in.

"Not yet," the tall guy said, following Morgan into the house.

"Jesus. You're all such Debbie Downers," I said as I closed the door.

"We're realists, Ms. True. You have threats against you, and we are taking them very seriously."

"Fine. I'm worried too. You're right. But we don't have to go over the top here."

While I stood there, half dressed, redness crept up my chest.

I'd never been that girl.

"Over the top would've been if we came in with our guns out, ma'am," the tall man said.

I shook my head as I walked back toward the couch. "Men. You're all crazy." I collapsed onto the cushion.

"We're going to survey the perimeter while Morgan checks the house. We'll be out of your hair shortly," Thomas reassured me before he walked toward the back door.

"The sooner the better." I crossed my arms over my chest.

"I'm staying," Morgan told me as he set his feet shoulder-width apart, puffing himself out like a cat.

"No, you're not." I shot up and moved toward him.

I wanted him to stay—not because he had to, but because he wanted to.

He peered down at me. "Yes. I. Am."

"Why?" I glared at him.

His eyes darted toward my chest, and my eyes followed. For the love of God, my arms had pushed my breasts up, putting them on full display.

When I brought my eyes back to his, he was still gawking at my chest. Any embarrassment I'd had vanished. Morgan DeLuca wanted seconds. Or would it be thirds?

"Because I won't be able to sleep tonight if I think someone is attacking you."

"I have a gun."

He closed his eyes, pinching the bridge of his nose. "That doesn't put my mind at ease, princess."

I cocked my head. "Why? 'Cause I'm a girl?"

"No, Race. Let me check out the house and have a quick meeting with the guys, and I'll explain it to you."

I rolled my eyes, turning my back to him. Before I took two steps, his hand wrapped around my arm, dragging me backward.

"Excuse me," I snapped, staring at his hand.

"Listen, Race. Drop the attitude for five fucking minutes. I'm here to protect you. You can wait." He touched my chin, raising my eyes to meet his glare. "Don't get all huffy and stomp off like a child. Please let me do my job without any backtalk, woman."

"Go," I said as I shooed him away. "Do your job." I cringed, knowing that it sounded crappy.

He released my arm as his jaw tightened. "Stay here." He pointed to the floor.

I crossed my arms again. "Fine."

He marched off, moving from room to room.

Why in the hell did Morgan DeLuca make the strong businesswoman in me disappear?

When I was around him, I turned into a bitch, a drunk, or a loose-lipped woman.

"Find anything good?" I called out, still standing in the same spot.

"Nope." He stalked into the kitchen, slamming the back door as he left.

I tiptoed to the kitchen, opened the blinds, and watched them. They were huddling together in the sand. No matter how hard I tried, I couldn't make out what they were saying to each other. When they broke apart and Morgan started to walk back up the steps, I ran back to my spot.

When he walked into the room, he stared at me with his eyebrow cocked. "You stayed?"

"Yes."

He narrowed his eyes at me. "Doesn't matter. The perimeter is clear and no one is inside the house. The guys have gone back home."

"Can I move now?"

"Yes."

I turned my back, moving faster this time, and fell on the couch. "I could've told you that no one was here. You didn't need to bring the guys over to check. Now that I'm safe, you can go. Your job doesn't entail guarding me." I grabbed the remote, flipped through the channels, and tried not to look at him.

He sat down, turning to glare at me. "I'm staying with you."

I stared back. "Why? You just said no one is here."

"I want to make sure you're safe tonight."

"Isn't that going above the call of duty?"

He pinched the bridge of his nose, letting out a long, hard breath. "Race," he said, peering up at me, "you're more than a job to me. Didn't the other night mean anything to you?"

"Well, I..." I mumbled, feeling like a complete asshole.

He leaned forward, resting his elbows on his knees and raking his fingers through his hair. "It meant something to me. You weren't just a one-night stand. And until I know who's after you, I'm not chancing anything happening to you. We've been over this before. Can you stop being a hard-ass for five minutes?"

"I'm sorry." I scooted closer to him. "I was going to watch a movie before bed. Do you want to watch a movie?" I asked, swallowing hard and trying to avoid temptation.

"Whatever you want." He leaned back into the couch cushion.

"*Stepmom* or *P.S. I Love You*?" Luckily for him, I had them both on DVD.

"Which one has the most action?"

I threw my head back against the cushion and smirked. "*P.S.* has more death."

"Sounds good."

"Popcorn?" I got up from the couch just as the previews started.

"Want my help?" He started to stand.

I pushed him down. "I got it. You relax."

I tossed the popcorn in the microwave and stared at it as it turned, popping slowly.

I wanted him again. Having him this close, I wanted to feel his skin against me as his mouth covered mine.

Lost in thought, I stood on my tiptoes and reached for a glass bowl. I touched the bottom edge, trying to coax it out. As if in slow motion, the bowl came barreling out of the cupboard and began to fall.

"Fuck." I flinched as I tried to grab it. As it hit the edge of the counter, it shattered, crashing to the floor in pieces, shards of glass trailing in its wake.

Before I could blink, Morgan was standing by my side, pulling me away from the wreckage of the bowl.

I jumped, yelping loudly. "Jesus, you scared the shit out of me."

"Sorry." He lifted me away from the glass.

"Damn it," I whispered as I caught a glimpse of my hands.

He pulled my hands closer. "Let me see."

Instead of pulling back, I gave in.

Blood had already began to pool in my palms and dripped from the edges.

Why did I have to try to catch the fucking bowl?

"The cuts don't look too deep." He brought my hands closer to his face and inspected them. "We need to clean the wounds and stop the bleeding."

"Are you a doctor now?" I tried to choke down the tears that were threatening to fall.

He grabbed my waist and hoisted me onto the countertop. Shocked by his strength, I just gawked at him. We stared at each other as he brushed his thumbs against my stomach, causing my insides to flip.

"Just sit there and look pretty while I bandage you up."

He thinks I'm pretty.

I felt my cheeks flush.

His muscles moved under the edges of his T-shirt sleeves, and I became transfixed by their rhythm, squeezing my legs together. "This may hurt a little." He rubbed the soap into the paper towel.

I winced, trying to pull my hands back. "Isn't there a better way to do it?" I asked.

He stepped forward, almost standing between my legs.

My heart stopped and my breathing faltered.

"I just need to clean the blood away and make sure there are no shards inside the wounds before I bandage them."

"What are you doing?" My eyes grew wide.

He glanced up and grinned. "I'm standing where I know you can't kick me in the balls."

I sighed, resting my knees against his sides.

Might as well enjoy myself.

He touched my hand and pulled my fingers flat. I grimaced, waiting for the soap to sting. As he wiped my palm, the coolness of the water felt better than I'd expected.

Maybe my brain was fuzzy from him being so near, but I didn't feel pain. My belly fluttered as he touched me.

If I leaned forward just a little bit more, I could kiss him and smell him.

"Did you just sniff me?" He peered up, holding my hand in his.

"No." I squirmed, squeezing my knees against his sides and instantly regretting our position.

"You smelled me." He looked back down with a grin.

I swallowed hard, feeling wetness pool between my legs.

"Leave your hand open to dry." He opened my right hand and repeated the process.

"Are we good?" I asked as he finished wiping the last cut. I was ready to hop down and put a little space between us.

"Yeah, but we need to bandage them up first. They're still bleeding, and if we don't, you'll get it everywhere."

"Great." I rolled my eyes. Why the fuck had I made my interior white?

"Your hands are going to be sore tomorrow." His hands rested on my thighs, scorching my skin. "Where's your first-aid kit?"

I should've shaved. "Fucking fabulous," I muttered. "In the master bathroom." I motioned toward the hallway.

"Stay put," he commanded, pointing at me.

I hunched my shoulders, placing my palms up. "Where am I going? I'm not bleeding all over my place."

He rubbed his forehead as he walked down the hallway and out of sight.

"Get your shit together, Race," I told myself before inhaling a long, deep breath. "You're a strong woman.

You're an executive. You don't have time for romantic entanglements." I blew the air out of my lungs and closed my eyes. "We'd never work anyway," I told myself as I thought back to Friday night.

"What wouldn't work?"

I jumped and closed my fists. "Damn it!" I shrieked as pain sliced through my hands.

"I didn't mean to scare you," he said, setting the first-aid kit on the counter.

"I'm just jumpy," I lied as I peered down at my hands, bouncing my heels off the cabinet. "I'm sorry."

"For what? I'm the one who scared you."

I held my palms out, showing him the mess I'd made. "You're going to have to clean them again." I tried to hide my smile, 'cause in reality I'd welcome him between my legs.

"It's not a big deal, princess," he said in a calm voice, shrugging.

"Tell me more about yourself, Morgan," I said, trying to think of something other than his body and mine together, naked, sweaty.

Fuck me, I was hopeless.

"Not much to tell, Race. I told you a lot about myself the day we met."

"No, you didn't. I want to know more than you were in the army. Are you from around here?" I knew he wasn't, but damn it, getting information from him wasn't easy.

"I grew up in Chicago and just moved here right before I started working on your case."

"I was there once. It's an amazing city. The shopping is spectacular."

"I guess so. I'm not much of a shopper." He threw the bloody paper towel into the sink.

"Yeah. I can see that."

"Is that a dig?" He glanced up at me with a gleam in his eye.

I shook my head. "No. You're just a man." God, I was such an asshole sometimes. "What brought you to Florida?"

"I came for a wedding and my cousin offered me a job."

"Which one is your cousin?"

"Thomas." He opened the first-aid kit and grabbed a bandage.

"I can see the resemblance." They were both beefy men and drop-dead gorgeous. "Why did you join the army?" I knew I was always tight-lipped about my past and life, but getting information out of him was like pulling teeth.

"I got into some trouble as a kid. Judge told me I either join up or spend some time behind bars."

"What did you do? Rob someone?" I pursed my lips.

"Something like that," he mumbled.

"Huh."

"I haven't always been a good guy, Race," he said as he covered my hand with the bandage.

"We all do dumb stuff when we're young."

"You're still young."

"When we're younger." I emphasized the last word. "What exactly did you do? I want to hear this."

"Why do you want to know?"

I bit the inside of my mouth and thought about how to answer his question. "I'm just making small talk."

"I'd rather—"

"Wait," I interrupted him. "I just want to know who you are as a person. I promise not to judge you."

"You've been judging me since the day you met me."

A lump formed in my throat. "I'm sorry. I'm not going to judge you. I just want to know more about you. We all have a past, Morgan."

"I'll tell you something if you share some of yourself with me."

"Me?" I asked, a little terrified.

"Yeah. It's only fair, Race."

"Okay. You're on, but you go first." I chickened out. I wanted to hear his big, dark secret about his past life before I'd divulge anything about myself.

He started to slather antibiotic salve across my palm, but I felt nothing, too distracted listening to him. "I got mixed up with the wrong kids in high school. It started off with small things and just being bored. Eventually, our reputation made it to some higher-ups in the neighborhood."

"Higher-ups?" I swallowed hard.

"Yeah. Chicago still has a lot of organized crime. One day, we ripped off a truck full of goods."

"A truck?" I looked down at him with my mouth hanging open.

"An entire truck filled with electronics. We needed to sell the shit quick so we wouldn't get caught. The fence we used told someone, who then told someone else, and it got back to the man running things in our neighborhood."

"That doesn't sound very good." I stared down at his hands as he touched me with such tenderness that I became fixated.

"We were scared shitless at first, but once we met with the guy, we were excited. We were kids and dumb as hell, but we thought it was a great opportunity. Naturally, we were wrong, and we ended up arrested about a year later."

"That doesn't make you a bad guy, Morgan. It makes you a stupid kid."

"Nah, baby. I'm a total asshole. I didn't join the military out of some code of honor. I signed up because I didn't want to sit in jail." He pulled my hand up to his face and blew on the wetness.

Shivers ran down my spine as his breath skidded across my skin. "That doesn't make you an asshole."

"No." He grinned. "I'm just one naturally. I'm not the nicest person."

I started to giggle. "Morgan, I'm a bitch. I embrace that side of me. As long as you know who you are, the rest doesn't matter. I don't think you're an asshole anyway."

"I have my moments, Race." He opened the bandage and placed it over my palm, covering the wound.

"We all do." I watched as he carefully covered my cuts, enthralled by his movements and the feel of him against me.

"All done." He patted my knees and rested his hands on my legs.

"Thank you," I whispered, trying to close my fists.

Crap. I'd be useless like this tomorrow.

Everything would be a fucking chore.

"What's wrong?" He tilted his head.

"I was just thinking." I bit my lip as I stared at him. "Tomorrow, my hands are going to hurt. What a pain in the ass."

He nodded as his thumb started to stroke the side of my kneecap. "Yeah. It'll take a few days until the pain subsides."

"Great." My body sagged. "This is the last thing I need."

"Take the day off tomorrow. It's probably best you don't go into work tomorrow anyway."

"Morgan, I can't skip work."

"When was the last time you had a day off?" He raised an eyebrow.

"Never. I'm a workaholic."

"Well, tomorrow, you're going to play hooky. With the new threat against you, it's better not to chance it." He squeezed my knee, sending tiny shock waves down my legs.

"I don't want some jerk to stop me. They'll think they won."

"Who gives a fuck what they think? If they think they won, they may get sloppy."

"I don't like it," I grumbled, shaking my head.

"Let's get you down," he said, placing his hands on my waist.

My eyes fluttered closed. My body reacted to his touch. I wanted more Morgan.

"I can get down," I said, placing my palms flat against the counter and instantly pulling them back. "Fuck."

"Woman, can't you let me help you without trying to do shit for yourself?" He increased the pressure of his fingertips against my sides.

"I'm not used to having someone help me." I frowned, wondering if I sounded strong or pitiful.

He lifted me in the air, and I tumbled forward, but I didn't dare use my palms to catch myself. I had a split second where I could've reached out and stopped myself, but I didn't.

His body felt nice against mine.

"Sorry," I whispered into his chest. I inhaled, getting another whiff of his cologne as his body shook with laughter.

"Go sit down, and I'll clean up in here," he said to me as I finally started to find my footing.

"Okay," I whispered.

I'm totally fucked.

I'd never let anyone get to me the way he did.

I could see us burning out in fantastic fashion.

I wondered if we'd be like a nuclear explosion, destroying everything in our path, including ourselves, or if the slow burn of need I felt would smolder like an ember, eventually extinguishing.

CHAPTER FOURTEEN

MORGAN

Chick Fuck

We sat in silence, our hands grazing each other's as we reached into the bowl.

A few times I got choked up, but I refused to let her see.

Why do women watch this depressing shit?

I hadn't expected it to be gut wrenching.

"I'm sorry I'm a mess." She sniffled, wiping her nose with the back of her hand.

"It's okay." I patted her knee, liking the softer side of Race, minus the hand thing. I leaned over and reached for a tissue. "Here." I handed it to her.

"It's just so sad," she said with a shaky voice as she took the tissues from my hand. She blew her nose with one and wiped her tears away with the other. "I can't get through this movie without using an entire box of Kleenex." She curled up next to me, snuggling into my side. "This part gets me every time." She wiped her face against my T-shirt.

I stroked her shoulder, letting my fingertips glide against her soft skin. Glancing down, I snuck a peek at her tits. Soft, round peaks stuck out of the top of her tank top, and I itched to taste them again.

"Are you watching?" She peered up at me, catching me staring at her chest.

I cleared my throat. "Yep."

"Watch," she demanded, lifting my chin to see the television instead of her breasts.

My eyes kept moving between the screen and her chest.

I couldn't help it.

I wanted her again.

As the final scenes closed and a new world of possibility opened for the female lead, the movie left me feeling...hopeful.

"Wasn't it amazing?" She wiped the last traces of tears off her face.

"It wasn't what I expected." Using the pad of my thumb, I brushed away a single tear that had been missed by her tissue. "Sorry," I whispered.

As I started to pull away, she said, "No. Don't."

My stomach instantly flipped. "Race," I warned, feeling my dick grow hard.

I knew what she was going to say. I could see it in her deep-green eyes. "Morgan, I can't stop thinking about us," she whispered as she touched my cheek.

"Me either." I pulled in a ragged breath.

"Stay with me tonight." She brushed her lips against my neck, sending shock waves rippling straight to my dick.

"I'm staying, princess. I told you that," I said, tangling my hand in her hair.

"No," she murmured against my skin. "I want you in my bed tonight."

I smirked, feeling my insides warm. "I'll stay wherever you want me to."

She crawled into my lap and held my face in her hands. "I want you to hold me tonight," she whispered, her eyes watery.

"Is that all?"

She shook her head, biting her bottom lip. "No. I want to feel you inside me again."

I grabbed her hips and squeezed them gently as she leaned forward and hovered over my lips.

"Please," she begged.

"I'll stay with you tonight. Not because I have to, Race, but because I want to." I captured her lips in a kiss.

She relaxed into me, wrapping her arms around my neck and kissing me back with fervor. My hands slid down her thighs, loving the feel of her soft skin against my palms.

I felt my restraint slipping as she moaned into my mouth. I slid her shorts to the side and touched the outside of her panties, feeling her body shudder in my arms.

Her legs widened, giving me access as I dipped my fingers underneath her panties, finding her already wet.

When my fingers glided over her clit, she moaned, "Yes," into my mouth.

I wanted her more than I had before. Remembering how it felt to sink myself deep inside of her, stroking her intimately, I didn't know if I could ever get enough of it.

Holding her back, I pushed two fingers inside her, instantly feeling her pussy clamp down. Positioning my thumb over her clit and using the same motion she'd used to get herself off, I worked my fingers in and out of her.

Her hand slid down my chest and palmed my dick through my jeans as I groaned. The deliciousness of it all had me hanging on by a thread. As her body grew tight, starting to milk my fingers, I withdrew.

"I. Need. Inside. You," I panted, lifting her in my arms as I stood. "Wrap your legs around me," I told her, carrying her toward her bedroom.

Her feet locked behind my back as she ground her pussy against my dick. "You're so hard," she whispered, repeating the motion.

"Hard for you, princess." I kicked her door open and carried her to her bed.

I laid her on the bed and pulled her shorts from her body. As they flew through the air, I planted my mouth against her and began to worship her with my mouth.

CHAPTER FIFTEEN

RACE

The Morning After

I tiptoed out of bed, trying not to wake him, dressing as I headed toward the kitchen.

I couldn't wipe the silly grin off my face, but I had to remember that this was nothing more than mutual attraction.

Morgan and I didn't have a future.

He hadn't promised me anything more, and I hadn't asked him to be mine.

As I grabbed the coffee pot to fill it with water, I hissed then pulled my hand back.

I stood here and glared at the empty pot. It took everything in me not to cry. Coffee was my elixir, and I felt like a zombie until I'd had at least one cup.

The floor creaked.

I glanced over, finding Morgan standing there.

"Morning," he said through a yawn, completely naked. His muscles tightened and his cock bobbed as he straightened.

Fuck me. The man was more beautiful in the daylight, every muscle taut and perfect.

"Morning," I whispered, my eyes glued to him. I swallowed hard, mesmerized.

"Need help?" He strode toward me, his cock waving.

I shook my head. "I can do it." I waved my hands.

He took a step closer, giving me a sleepy smile. "If you say so."

I reached for the coffee pot again.

I cringed as my hand slid around the handle, and I bit my lip. As I gritted my teeth, I carried it to the sink.

"Move over." He nudged my hip with his. "Let me do it."

I glared up at him. "I can do this."

"Race, you're sweating and your face is redder than an apple from carrying an empty pot. Let me do this. I've made coffee more times than I can count." His blue eyes twinkled, and his cock twitched. "Plus, I don't feel like waiting an hour for the first cup."

I rounded the island and took a seat on one of the barstools to get a better view. Watching him as he worked his magic on the coffee pot, I was enthralled by his nakedness.

"How did you know where I kept my coffee?"

He turned around to face me and leaned against the counter, pushing his cock farther out. "Lucky guess that you kept it in the cupboard above the pot. It's something most people do."

"Thanks for making it." I yawned against the back of my hand.

He pushed off the counter and his cock came toward me. "Let me take a look at your hands."

I tried to swallow, wishing I'd brushed my teeth before I'd left my room. "They're fine."

"Stop being so stubborn. I want to make sure they're healing. Last night, you couldn't stop moaning yes, and now you're back to your hard-ass self."

I straightened my back. "I'm just cranky until I get my coffee."

Overnight, the cuts had begun to scab and the blood had dried.

"You'd already have it if you would've let me make it to begin with." He cleared his throat. "We'll need to clean the dried blood off these, but they look good." He reached for the first-aid kit he'd left on the counter last night and pulled fresh bandages from the container. "First, let's have coffee, and then we'll clean them." He set the bandages off to the side. "It's best to give them some air for a little while."

"Yes, sir," I said to the side, blowing my nasty breath away from him.

"That's sexy." He chuckled quietly.

Before I could say anything, the pot beeped.

"Stay there, I'll grab you a cup." His eyes shifted to my shirt and the corner of his mouth twitched before he turned around.

I glanced down, noticing that my nipples were standing at attention. I tried to hide them, pulling my tank top away from my body, but it did nothing.

"How do you want your coffee?" He pulled two cups down, keeping his back to me.

I stared at his naked ass, studying it. "A dash of cream and two sugars, please," I mumbled.

His ass was as beautiful as the rest of him. The skin was blemish-free and smooth, sitting higher from the muscle tone. I'd say one thing about the military: It did a body good.

"Did you let work know you weren't coming in today?" He turned around and caught me as I gawked at him.

Slowly, I dragged my eyes up to his. "Yeah." I tried not to glance at his dick as he set the coffee in front of me.

I looped my fingers through the handle, holding it loosely. "You can go whenever you want. I'm just going to chill on the couch and get some work done." I kept my eyes down, peeking at him through my veiled eyelashes. Which, coincidently, were about crotch level.

"I'm going wherever you are," he said, setting his cup down.

"For the love of God," I said, but he lifted an eyebrow.

"I'm not going anywhere. So drop it. Why don't we do something today? You can work here later."

"I really need to work," I lied. I didn't know if I could spend the day in his presence without ending up in bed with him again.

"I won't keep you out long. I don't know the area well." He leaned forward, resting his hands against the counter. "You could show me around a little bit. Your hands need time to rest anyway."

"Are you sure that's a good idea?" I peeked at him from under my eyelashes.

"We'll call it a workday. I need to pick your brain a little."

I chewed my lip. "As long as it's for work. I don't want to keep you from doing your job."

"Race, no one can make me do what I don't want to. Finish your cup and then you're mine."

I wished his statement were true. "Where to first?"

"I need to stop at my place for a change of clothes."

"You can shower here."

"With you?" He grinned, running his thumb across his chin.

"If you want," I blurted out. The truth was that I wanted him to. Sitting here, watching him saunter around nude, threw my body into overdrive.

He walked around the counter, holding his hand out to me. "Oh, I want. Let's get your pretty ass wet."

I swallowed hard, wishing I could press my legs together to squash the familiar ache that amplified with his words. As I stood, sliding my hand into his, I rose up on my tiptoes and kissed him.

"Someday, you'll admit you want me for more than just my cock," he teased, brushing his nose against mine.

When I started to walk away, he smacked me on the ass, the echo reverberating through my kitchen.

"That's for being difficult."

I yelped, jumping from the impact and rubbing my ass as he followed me to the shower.

CHAPTER SIXTEEN

MORGAN

The Real Race True

"What are you looking at?" I walked out of my bedroom, slipping on a fresh shirt.

"Is this your mother?" She glanced over her shoulder.

"Yeah, that's Ma."

I hadn't had time to decorate, but I had placed a couple of photos around the room. I'd made sure to put a picture of Ma out. I knew that, as soon as she made it to Florida, she'd drop by and take note.

"Does she live here?" Her fingertips swept across the glass as she tilted her head.

I plucked the photo from her hands and placed it back on the coffee table. "She followed me here."

"That's so sweet." She turned and started to wander around my place.

"I guess so."

"Seriously. I have no one. That's why I'm so devoted to my work. It's the only thing I have in my life anymore."

I frowned, wondering how someone got to that point in their life. "That's sad, Race."

"I know." She traced the curves of the couch as her eyes roamed. "You don't have much here."

"I just moved in. I'm still trying to get everything set up."

She stopped and faced me, clasping her hands together. "I can help with that."

"You want to decorate?" I shuddered. Fuck. I hated shopping.

"I'm pretty good at it." She shrugged, plastering an innocent smile on her face. "What else do you have planned today?" She stepped closer.

If I had my way, I'd have her bent over the sofa and screaming my name within ten minutes. "I don't even know where to go around here."

"I'll take you, but only if I drive." She held her hand out, waiting for me to give her the keys.

The woman must've lost her marbles.

No one, and I mean no one, would drive my girl. She was a Dodge Challenger SRT Hellcat. Not only was she gorgeous, she could kick serious ass.

I shook my head, crossing my arms over my chest. "No one but me drives Elvira."

She burst out laughing, holding her stomach. "Elvira?" She rolled her eyes. "You've got to be shitting me."

I puffed my chest out, setting my lips in a firm line. "It's the perfect name for my girl."

Covering her mouth, she tried to calm her giggles. "I don't think I've ever known anyone who named their car Elvira. You've got to tell me why." Her hand dropped.

Rubbing the back of my neck, I cleared my throat. "Well, I've never slept with an Elvira. I wouldn't want to be reminded of someone from my past every day when I climbed into her. Plus, when I was a kid, I used to be mesmerized by her. When I saw my black beauty, I knew the name fit. She was sleek, sexy, and dark."

Her smile vanished. "Makes sense when I hear you say it. I don't know many guys who would admit that Elvira was their childhood crush." She shrugged.

"I'll drive." I grabbed the keys off the kitchen counter.

Before I could close my fist, she plucked them from my hands. "Gotta get them back from me if you want to drive." She moved quickly, giggling as she sprinted to the other side of the room.

"Race," I said, grabbing my head, "come on."

She dangled the keys from her fingers and shook them.

"Woman," I said, dropping my hands to my sides, "no one fucks with Elvira."

"I'll be gentle."

I stalked toward her, ready to snatch the keys from her fingertips.

She darted to the right, but I reached out, grabbed her arm, and spun her around to face me. Caging her in when she collided with the wall, I placed my arms on either side of her.

I closed my eyes, trying to steady my breathing and not think about her beautiful tits being within inches of my mouth. We'd never get out of here. "Can we be adults, princess?"

When her body began to move, I opened my eyes.

"Jesus Christ," I muttered as she placed the keys down her shirt and nestled them between her breasts.

"What are you going to do now?" She grinned, raising one eyebrow.

"Babe, you think that's going to stop me from getting them?" My eyes dipped to her chest, and I studied its beauty. I'd use my fucking teeth if I had to.

"I hope not." She smirked, blinking slowly.

"I thought we were going to keep today all business?" I asked, swallowing hard and trying not to face-plant in her cleavage.

"I think that went out the window this morning in the shower." She laughed softly.

Without saying another word, I pulled her to me and stared down into her deep-green eyes. Her breath hitched as I brought my lips down on hers and kissed her hard.

The sounds of our breathing filled the room as our mouths tried to devour each other. Her hands slid up my arms, leaving goose bumps in their path, before she grabbed the hair on top of my head and held me to her.

I grabbed her arms and pried her from me before my lips broke contact. "We can't," I said, my voice sounding winded as it cracked.

Wrinkles lined her forehead as she gawked at me. "Why not?"

"We'll never get out of here."

She sucked her lip in her mouth as her head fell forward. "Can't get enough of me?"

"I don't know if I'll ever get enough of you."

"You won't?" Her eyes grew wide.

I closed my eyes, drawing in a deep breath through my nose. "I wouldn't just fuck you to fuck you, Race."

"You don't have to lie to me, Morgan." Pushing against my chest, she put space between us.

"Listen," I said as I dragged my hands through my hair, "it's been a long time since I've liked anyone. I really like you. Lord knows why, because you can be a pain in the ass at times." I smiled, hoping she'd know I was joking. "I'm supposed to protect you and find out who is threatening you, not fuck you every chance I get."

"I started it." She glanced down at her feet. "I'll behave," she said as she pulled my keys from her shirt. "Here." The keys dangled from her fingertips.

I rubbed my forehead, feeling like the biggest tool. This girl had me in knots. She'd scrambled my brain in a few short days. I knew I was fucked.

"You keep them. I'll let you drive Elvira."

"Really?"

"Yes."

Twirling the keys in her fingers, she whistled before she yelled, "Yes."

"I see you're happy."

"Totally worth kissing you to be able to drive that baby."

"You didn't want to kiss me?" I felt my stomach plummet.

"Oh, I did, but I didn't think you'd let me drive the car. Let's hit the road." She started for the door.

I followed behind her, dragging my feet. "Let's set a few ground rules first."

She'd already climbed inside Elvira before I'd finished the sentence. "She'll be fine." She slammed the door.

Looking up at the sky, I cursed. I could swear God was trying to punish me.

Thomas had to give Race to me as my first case. It couldn't have been something easy, like a cheating spouse? No. I'd had to get the overbearing, ballbusting corporate executive who made my dick feel like a lead pipe ready to break off.

Before I settled in my seat, she had the car started and revved the engine. "Ground rules," I reminded her.

"Hit me." She gripped the steering wheel and looked like a woman possessed.

"Don't your hands hurt?"

"I was so excited to get behind the wheel that I totally forgot." She shrugged, easing her grip.

"Number one, go the speed limit. Two, no changing lanes unnecessarily, and three, be kind to my girl." I sounded like my mother rattling off commands when I'd started to drive.

I had hit asshole territory.

"I can do that," she said as she started to back up.

I fastened my seat belt and said a small prayer as I shifted in my seat.

As she put the car in drive, the wheels began to screech, causing the car to fishtail. I reached for the dashboard, my heart pounding wildly as I screamed, "Race."

"What?" she asked innocently as she glanced at me.

The car glided across the pavement, not gripping the surface.

She turned the wheel, gaining control of Elvira. "Did I ever tell you how I got my name?"

"No." I braced myself. "Slow the hell down though."

"We're good. My daddy was a huge fan of racing. He named me Race because of it. When I was a little girl, he'd take me to some of the dirt courses around here and let me speed around. I could barely see over the damn steering wheel, but I drove like a speed demon."

"Shocking."

"I could've gone pro if I'd stuck with it."

"I can't breathe." I wiped the sweat from my forehead.

"Oh, stop being such a baby. Elvira couldn't be in better hands."

When the car came to a screeching halt at the end of my street, I was ready to run out of the car and lie down in front of it just to get her to stop.

"This is the only thing I have in my name. I don't want you to fuck her up, princess."

"I promise to behave if you calm down." She looked over at me.

"Why don't I believe you?"

Using her fingers, she made an X over her heart. "I promise." Her lips parted, giving me a toothy and totally bullshit smile.

I should've demanded the keys back.

The car behind us honked, causing Race to flip them off in the rearview mirror.

My mouth fell open. "What's gotten into you?"

"It's this car. I swear I turn into a different person when I'm behind the wheel of a car with some power."

"Just go before you start shit and I have to finish it." I motioned for her to move, keeping my eyes glued to the side mirror. The last thing I wanted to do was kick someone's ass before we had even driven a mile.

She looked like a different person today.

The tank top and skinny jeans looked good on her. She looked calmer and more relaxed than I'd ever seen her. The way she held the leather wheel in her hands made it clear that she was in her element.

As she eased onto the street without causing the car to spin, I took a deep breath and tried to relax. "So why don't you race anymore?"

"When my father died, I didn't want to go to the course anymore. I miss him every day, but I just couldn't go there. I started to study harder and decided to leave that world behind."

"I'm sorry. What happened to him, if you don't mind my asking?" I watched her face change.

I knew the trauma of losing a parent. My dad hadn't died, but the bastard might as well have, since he'd dropped off the face of the Earth.

"He was hit by a semi and died instantly." Her chin trembled. "It was my fault."

I blinked. "Race, how could it be your fault?"

"It just is. Ask my mama. She'll tell you." She shrugged.

"She can't feel that way. How old were you?"

"Twelve." She tightened her grip on the steering wheel.

"You can hardly be at fault," I reassured her, placing a hand on her shoulder. "You were just a little kid."

"Anyway, he was my best friend and we spent our weekends together at the racetrack."

"You know you aren't at fault, Race, right?" I asked, concerned about her change of attitude.

"In my heart I know it, but I can still hear the words coming out of my mama's mouth."

"Sometimes parents say shit they don't mean," I said, knowing that my ma had said more than a few things I knew she wished she could take back.

"I know," she said, keeping her eyes on the road.

She weaved in and out of traffic, and I couldn't look. "It's quite a leap from race car driver to the corporate world." I swallowed hard, trying to get the lump out of my throat.

"I wanted something challenging and cutthroat, but I never expected what's happening now."

As she pulled into the IKEA parking lot, my phone rang and Thomas's number scrolled across the radio.

"Let me grab this. Thomas may have some news." I pulled my phone out of my pocket and took it off Bluetooth.

"Yeah?" I asked, hoping he had a lead.

"I think I found him," Thomas said, the excitement in his voice evident. "Come to the office this afternoon and we'll work out a game plan."

CHAPTER SEVENTEEN

RACE

Problem

"We'll be in shortly. Thanks, man." Morgan glanced at me as I pulled my phone from my purse, needing to check my messages. "He has a lead," he whispered, covering the phone with his hand.

"Thank God," I mumbled, glancing down at my screen.

My hands began to shake as I checked my messages. I squeezed my eyes shut, trying to slow my breathing. I swallowed down the bile that had started to rise in my throat.

> **Race,**
> **The time is coming. Meet me tomorrow at 7 p.m. if you want your tape back. Come alone or I'll e-mail it to your boss. I bet he'd like to hear you moaning like a whore.**

I couldn't read any more.

I couldn't breathe.

"We'll stop in the office later. We're doing a few things today." There was a long pause. "Yeah, I have her with me. You told me to keep an eye on her." More silence. "Don't worry, man. I got it."

I turned my phone off and tossed it back in my purse.

"Looks like we're a step closer to solving your case," he said.

"Thank God," I replied, knowing that either way, it would be over tomorrow night.

"Ready to do some shopping?" Morgan asked.

Pulling at my lip, I stared at him as he spoke but didn't hear the words.

"Race." He touched my leg as his forehead scrunched.

I blinked a few times, trying to clear my head. "Sorry. I zoned out." I couldn't look at him.

"What's wrong? You look pale."

"I'm just hungry," I lied.

"You want to skip shopping and go grab some lunch?" he asked as his thumb stroked my knee.

I shook my head, still not making eye contact. "No. Let's shop and then we'll grab a bite to eat."

In my heart, I knew I should tell him about the e-mail. He needed to handle things and get the video from the bastard who had threatened me, but I couldn't risk everything going to shit and it landing in the hands of my boss.

But I wasn't ready to ruin our day together.

"Okay, Race. This is your show. I'm fine with the few items I have, but have at it."

"You need to make it more like a home." I finally brought my eyes to his.

"I'm a simple guy. A couch and a television are all I need to survive."

"Just let me get lost in a little shopping today. What's my budget?" I rubbed my hands together. I pushed all thoughts of tomorrow night out of my mind, focusing on Morgan.

Tomorrow I'd go there, retrieve the video, and be done with it.

It was that simple.

Everything would finally be over.

My life could return to normal.

"I'm not giving you a total. Let's see what you find and we'll go from there."

Retail therapy would help. Lots of retail therapy. "If you say I have one hundred dollars, I'm going to throw myself into traffic."

He reached in his back pocket and pulled his wallet out. "Let me see how much I have." He opened it, turned it upside down, and shook it until a few bills fell into his lap. "I have one hundred and seventeen dollars. Dazzle me with your ability."

"For fuck's sake." I rolled my eyes.

He stuffed the money back in his wallet. "I have a credit card, princess."

"Thank God. I know the military doesn't pay well, though, so I don't want to go crazy."

"I think I can handle anything you throw at me. It's IKEA anyway. I could probably decorate my entire place for one hundred and seventeen dollars."

"Hardly," I scoffed as I threw the keys at him. "It adds up quickly."

"Show me your mad skills." He smiled. "Hey, thanks for not wrecking Elvira."

"I would never. I can't wait to drive her home. Now, let's go spend your money."

"After you," he said as I climbed out of the car and gently closed the door. As we entered the store, his mouth fell open. "Holy shit."

"What's wrong?"

"We're going to be here all day."

"Nah. We'll make it quick. What do you need?"

"I don't know," he said as he followed behind me.

"Don't worry. We'll figure it out as we go," I reassured him, happy that I'd be able to lose myself in the wonders of IKEA.

"I'm all yours."

My chest tightened at his words.

I have a problem.

I liked Morgan.

No, that wasn't totally true.

I wanted Morgan.

Strike that.

I had a crush on Morgan.

Spending time with him had made me want him more. The moment I'd met him, I'd felt my attraction to him, but I tried to tell myself that it was only physical.

"I'm all yours," he repeated as he grabbed a cart.

He made me want to go back on the promise I'd made of swearing off relationships forever.

CHAPTER EIGHTEEN

MORGAN

Plans

I still hated shopping.

Even with Race by my side.

I hated every damn minute of it.

I bought shit I didn't need because she said that it was cute.

What use did I have for decorative pillows for my bed? I never even made the damn thing, let alone decorated it.

"Thanks for lunch and the drink," she said as we pulled into the parking lot of ALFA PI.

"You seemed on edge. I thought you could use a little something."

"I just get more nervous with each passing day." Her eyes didn't meet mine when she spoke. "You think you guys have a solid lead?" She still seemed distant.

She was hiding something.

Her playful attitude from earlier had vanished.

She'd played it off like nothing happened, but I could tell.

"We won't be here long." I placed my hand on hers. "I just want to see what Thomas found."

"It doesn't matter. I've decided to not work at all today. I'm not even going to look at my phone."

Alarm bells started to ring in my head.

"Race, is there something you aren't telling me?"

Race had been glued to her phone during business hours.

"Everything is fine," she reassured me as we walked toward the building.

"Hey, Morgan," Angel greeted us.

"Hey, Angel. Is Thomas in his office?" I placed my hand on the small of Race's back just because I could.

Race didn't try to escape my touch—she stood still at my side.

"Yeah. He's expecting you. Go on back." Angel's eyes dropped to my arm.

"Thanks." I guided Race down the hallway, my hand still on her lower back. "All the way at the end."

"I remember." She walked slow enough to keep the contact between us. "Who is she?"

I looked down at Race, confused. "Who? Angel?"

She looked away, staring down the hallway. "Yes."

"She's Thomas's girl."

She was jealous.

"Oh," she said as her eyebrows shot up. "Well, that's nice."

I stopped walking, turning her body toward me. "Are you jealous, Race?"

"No." She shook her head but still not looking me in the eye.

"Do you always lie so much?"

She crossed her arms, becoming defensive. "No," she snapped, finally glancing up at me.

"Sure. But I know when you're not telling me the truth."

She gnawed on her lip. "Can we drop it?" she asked, moving her hands to her sides.

When we arrived at the door, I leaned forward, invading her personal space. "You're hiding something, and I need to know what it is. I expect you to tell me when we're done meeting with Thomas."

Her eyes dropped to the floor as her shoulders sagged. "Okay," she whispered as I opened his door.

"Hey, T," I greeted him, helping Race sit before I took the seat next to her. "Find anything out?"

He turned his attention to his computer. "I was able to figure out the name of his cousin using an obituary and college records. I haven't moved past that yet. His name is—"

A knock on the door caused him to stop mid-sentence. "Thomas," a voice said from the other side.

"Come in, Sam," Thomas called out.

I turned to catch a glimpse of the infamous Sam.

Sam slid the sunglasses to the top of his head as he looked around the room. "Sorry. I didn't mean to interrupt." He was a tower of a man, with wide shoulders, cropped hair, and a fit physique.

Thomas walked toward Sam with an extended hand. "You aren't. Sam, this is Morgan, another member of ALFA PI."

Sam gave me a quick nod. "Nice to meet you, Morgan."

"Sam." I returned the nod.

"I'm excited to start working. It's great to be home again."

"I didn't think I'd be able to lure you away from New Orleans," Thomas told him as he placed a hand on his shoulder. "Is Fiona settled?"

"Yeah. She's excited for a fresh start." Sam peered over his shoulder. "Is James here?"

"He's in his office, I believe."

Sam fidgeted with the file in his hands. "I need to talk to him."

"Go ahead. Don't worry. He's cooled down in the last couple of years."

"I'd hope so." Sam gave Thomas a weak smile. "I'm going to go have a chat with James and then get settled in my office."

"I'll come looking for you when we're done here. We need to discuss some things," Thomas told him as he held the door open.

"Nice to meet you, Morgan. You too, ma'am."

"Race."

"Race," he repeated before he closed the door.

Thomas laughed, plopping down in his chair. "This is going to be fun."

"Sure will be."

"Where was I?" Thomas asked as he scratched his head.

"The name." I glanced at Race.

She wasn't herself.

She'd been entirely too quiet for the last hour.

"Tyler O'Shea."

"Race, does that sound right?"

She seemed uninterested. "Yeah. I think so."

"I'll do some digging and see what I can come up with." I stood, holding my hand out to Race. "Thanks for getting the name for me, Thomas."

She placed her tiny palm in mine and I closed my fingers around her hand, helping her up from the chair.

"Morgan, can I talk to you in private for a moment?" Thomas asked.

Race glanced up.

"Go wait for me in my office. I'll be right there," I whispered to her.

She gave me a brief nod and left.

"What's up, Thomas?" I asked as I sat back down.

"What's going on with you two?"

"Nothing," I lied, shaking my head.

"I saw how you touched her. There's something different about you two. And what the hell happened to her hands?"

"Listen." I rubbed the back of my neck, "you told me to stay with her to make sure she was safe last night. I did that."

"I also asked you to keep it in your pants, but did you do that too?" he asked, tilting his head to the side.

"Well, um, no. I didn't listen to that part. But—"

"Just get the case solved," he told me, crossing his arms in front of his chest.

"I will."

"Shopping? Really?"

"Yeah, man. She mocked my place and said I needed to decorate. She couldn't work today because she cut her hands when a bowl shattered last night. We thought it was best if she gave her hands a day to heal."

"Uh-huh," he mumbled.

I flipped him off, closed the door, and headed to my office.

As I passed James's door, I heard heated words being exchanged. I guessed not everything was water under the bridge when it pertained to Izzy.

Race had sprawled out on the small love seat. Her arm was resting against her face, her mouth slightly parted, and her legs crossed at her ankles.

I sat down, turning my computer on. "Sorry about that."

"It's okay," she whispered without moving.

"Why don't you tell me what's on your mind, princess?"

She didn't look at me. "I got another message today while you were talking to Thomas," she said, hiding behind her arm.

I froze, knowing that she'd hid it for a reason. "Fuck. What did it say?"

"I didn't read it all. Something about come alone and he wanted to meet me tomorrow."

"You're not going."

She glared at me. "It's my career, Morgan."

"I don't care what it is, Race. You're *not* going to put your life in danger. I'll get the tape for you."

"How?"

"I'm going to get my ass up and find everything I can on Tyler O'Shea. Then I'm going to get the guys together and we're going to form a plan. You are not going. I won't allow it. End of story."

"Morgan," she said before I pinned her with my eyes.

I shook my head, glaring at her. "Absolutely not."

"It's my life hanging in the balance."

"Woman, if I have to tie your ass to the bed, you're not going."

"Fine," she said, crossing her arms over her chest.

"I'm glad you're seeing things my way," I said, smirking.

"You can be a jerk," she snarled.

"I told you I was an asshole sometimes."

She didn't reply as I sat down and started researching Tyler O'Shea.

He lived in Tampa and had gotten married three years ago to a woman named Natasha. Both held business degrees, and Tyler worked at a financial firm in the area.

The thing I hadn't expected was where Natasha worked.

She had become employed two years ago with the same company Race worked for.

Her position in the company was lower, but she was in line for the same promotion as Race. If Tyler was able to destroy Race's career, Natasha would be able to climb the corporate ladder quicker.

I stood without excusing myself, and I headed straight for Thomas's office.

"We have a problem." I walked through the door without knocking again.

I saw Angel bent over the desk with a look matching my own. "Oh my God. I'm so sorry." I covered my eyes, splaying my fingers so I could peek. "Fuck. Again," I muttered as I started to back up.

"Out," Thomas yelled, pointing toward the door.

"What's he all pissy about?" James asked from behind me as I closed the door.

"He was a little busy when I walked in." I motioned toward Thomas's office. "They sure get a lot of use out of that desk."

He looked at the ceiling and shook his head. "I've told him a million times to lock the damn door. I've seen way more of him than I ever wanted to lately." James chuckled.

"Don't you knock?"

"Nah. I kind of like catching them. I think they like it too, or else he'd lock the damn door."

"Interesting." I scrubbed my hand across my face. "Can I talk to you, since Thomas is busy?"

"Step into my office and we'll chat until he's done. Don't worry. He's quick."

I followed him inside and took a seat on the couch.

Before I could speak, Thomas's door opened and closed.

"See." James motioned toward the hallway. "Quick."

"Poor girl." I snickered.

"What can I do for you?" James asked as he sat down in the leather chair across from me.

"It's about this case. I need extra eyes and hands on deck tomorrow. Do you know anything about her case?"

"I know about all the cases in the office. What's happening tomorrow?"

I spent the next five minutes explaining the e-mail that she'd received today and the background information on Tyler O'Shea.

He leaned forward, resting his elbows on his knees. "Here's what we're going to do. I'll put Sam on staking out Tyler and updating us on his movements. Thomas and I will decide the best course of action on our end, and we'll have extra bodies at the meeting point tomorrow night."

"They'll stay out of sight though, right?" I asked, my leg shaking. If this went south, it would all fall on my shoulders.

"No one will see us. You stay by Race's side until we have the douchebag and the tape in our hands."

"That may be a problem."

"Why?" His face contorted.

"She's pissed at me right now. It's going to be hell to convince her to let me stick by her side and let us handle everything."

Pinching the bridge of his nose, he leaned back in the chair and stretched his legs out. "Is there something going on with you two?" he asked.

"Well..." I winced.

"Does she like you?"

"Yes."

"Do you like her?"

"Yes."

"Make sure she doesn't want to get rid of you tonight. Keep her close. Take her to dinner. Buy her some drinks. Do something. Just don't let her out of your sight."

"Gotcha, buddy. Text me the details and keep me updated. I'm going to get Race and head out. Thanks for your help."

"I'll message you later, after I figure everything out and get it all set up. Remember, only worry about your client."

"Shit's easier said than done." I walked toward the door.

Just then there was a small knock. "Jimmy," Izzy said in a low tone.

"Looks like you better lock your door." I opened the door to my cousin, who was standing there with her fist up and about to knock.

"Hey, Morgan."

"Iz. Go easy on him."

"If we don't come out in thirty minutes, call the paramedics," she said as she walked past me and into his office.

"I'll let you two have some time alone."

"Thanks." James looked around Izzy. "Lock the door, love," he said as the door started to close.

I shook my head, wondering how I was the only person in the office not getting any at-work action.

Then again, I was the only one in the office who wasn't attached.

"Race," I called out as I opened the door and walked into my office, ready to head outside. My heart jumped into my throat when I noticed the couch empty—Race was gone.

I marched into the waiting room where Angel sat, fixing her makeup in a small compact mirror. "Where is she?" I asked, squeezing my fists at my sides.

"She just walked out a minute ago. She needed some air," Angel replied, wiping the corners of her lips.

"Fuck," I muttered, smashing through the front doors in a panic. "Race," I called out as I looked around, shielding my eyes from the sun.

She was standing next to Elvira, her pale skin whiter than normal. She didn't reply, just stood like a statue looking down.

"Race." I jogged toward her. "What's wrong?"

She pointed toward the ground. "Elvira," she whispered.

Someone had slashed my tires. Each one had huge punctures, and enough air had seeped out of them that they were practically flat.

"Fuck!" I yelled, feeling my chest tighten. I wasn't upset about the car. It was just an object. If she had come out just a few minutes earlier... I couldn't think about it.

"I'm so sorry," she whispered, clutching her neck. "It's all my fault."

"It's just a car." I tried to keep my voice calm as I put my arm around her. "It can be fixed. It's not your fault."

She held a tiny piece of paper out. "Yes, it is. Look."

"'You can't save her. Keep your nose where it belongs,'" I read out loud, pulling her closer to me.

Whoever this prick was, he sure had balls as big as basketballs. To come to this office and slash my tires was extremely risky.

"Shh. It's no big deal. You're safe and that's all that matters."

Her shoulders shook as tears began to stream down her face. "I'm so sorry," she repeated, sucking in a shaky breath.

"It's only a car, princess."

Her body could've had the note for me instead of it being left on Elvira.

"Let me help you fix it," she whispered as she peered up at me.

"I'm sure Thomas has insurance for stuff like this." I could see that there were dangers to this job that I hadn't anticipated.

"I know a guy I can call."

"You know a guy?" My eyes narrowed. "Sounds ominous."

"An old racing contact of my dad's. Let me call him, please." She batted her eyelashes.

Fuck.

There was no way I could refuse her.

"Okay. Let's go inside, and you can call him while I speak with Thomas."

She nodded and leaned into my side. "We'll get your baby back in action."

"I can get a rental until she's all fixed up. Stop worrying."

"Everything okay?" Angel asked as we walked back inside.

"Yeah, Angel. Everything will be okay." I gave her a fake smile, my insides turning about what had transpired. I glanced down at Race. "Go in my office and use the phone while I speak with Thomas."

She nodded and walked down the hallway. I watched, completely transfixed by the sway of her hips. Before she opened the door, she looked over her shoulder and caught me.

"See something you like, big boy?" Angel asked from my side.

My face flushed. "I wanted to make sure she went to the right door. I wouldn't want her walking in on something she shouldn't." I arched an eyebrow and didn't bother to hide my amusement as her nose scrunched.

She coughed, "Asshole."

"Is Thomas alone?"

"As far as I know." She busied herself with the stack of paperwork at her desk.

I marched down the hallway, straight to Thomas's office.

This time, I knocked.

"Come in."

"Sorry to interrupt, but I needed to talk with you about a situation."

"What's the problem now?" Thomas peered up from behind his desk.

I dragged my hands through my hair. "I went outside to find Race, and Elvira's tires were slashed."

"I'll get James on the parking lot surveillance video right away."

"Um," I mumbled, glancing behind me toward James's door, "he's kind of busy right now."

"What the fuck is he doing?" Thomas moved around the desk.

I put up my hands, stopping him from leaving. "Just give him a few minutes. What do I do about the car?"

"Just give me the bill and we'll pay it. Insurance will cover it."

"Thanks, Thomas."

"Don't thank me yet. Since you're here, we need to discuss your relationship with Ms. True." He leaned forward, resting his elbows on the desk. "James," he called out as he walked into the room, straightening his clothes. "Shut the door, James," Thomas said as he collapsed in his chair.

"Do I want to hear this?" I knew what he was peeved about.

"Listen, smartass. Dating a client can complicate shit and open us up to a slew of lawsuits."

I set my mouth in a firm line at the insinuation that she'd be after money. "Race isn't like that."

He shook his head, throwing his body back into the chair. "Be careful. You're in very dangerous territory."

"I know. I didn't mean for anything to happen."

Thomas crossed his arms in front of his chest. "I don't want excuses. Keep her safe and close the case."

"I never set out to like her. I don't know what happened, but I'll keep her safe. And the case should be over tomorrow. She just makes me crazy."

"Women do that." James toyed with the wedding ring on his hand.

"Firsthand knowledge?" My eyes dropped to his hand.

"I didn't want to like Izzy. God, she's such a pain in the ass. I couldn't help it. One thing led to another, and here I am. Married." He shook his head. "Sometimes we can't resist fate."

"Hey, James, Hallmark wants their cheesy line back," Thomas joked.

"Shut up, man." James lifted his chin to Thomas.

"Anyway, we'll handle everything," Thomas said. "Stay with her tonight. I don't like that this person came here and vandalized your car. They're bold and could try anything. Just, for the love of God, stay on your toes."

"I won't let my guard down."

"A dead client doesn't pay," James added.

Jesus. "You know just the right shit to make me feel better, James."

"James, I need you to pull the parking lot footage for the last hour," Thomas said, tapping his finger on the desk.

"What happened?" James raised an eyebrow as he glanced at me.

"Someone slashed my tires."

"Fuck." He pushed himself up from the chair. "I'm on it."

I closed my eyes, wishing I could fast-forward to tomorrow, when hopefully, all of this would be over. "Do you need me for anything else?" I asked, needing to get back to Race.

"No. We'll get everything set and send you the details."

"Okay. I'm going to call for a rental car and get Elvira towed."

"Sounds like a plan."

"Oh, and, Morgan," Thomas said as I had one foot in the hallway.

"Yeah?" I asked, keeping my back to him and closing my eyes.

"Thanks for knocking this time, man."

Everyone laughed.

CHAPTER NINETEEN

RACE

The Guy

"I have great news," I told Morgan as he sat down at his desk.

Rocking back and forth, he tried to muster a smile. "Hit me."

"Johnny is bringing new tires and he's going to fix Elvira in the parking lot."

"The guy?" he asked with a halfhearted grin.

I nodded, trying to contain my excitement. "The guy."

"That's great, princess." He held his hand out to me, a serious look on his face. "We gotta talk. It's about Tyler and the entire situation."

"Can I go tomorrow?" I held my breath.

"No."

I scowled, grinding my teeth.

"Do you trust me, Race?" He reached out for me.

This time, I didn't hesitate as I set my hand in his, finally giving in. "Yes."

"Good." He pulled me forward and wrapped his arms around me. "Then you aren't fucking going."

I tumbled into his lap and yelled, "Hey."

He positioned me in his lap, cocooning me against his torso.

I peered up at him, confused. "What are you doing?"

"Protecting you," he whispered in my ear.

My breath hitched.

For once, I was at a loss for words.

"I'm going to stay with you again tonight."

"You don't have to. I'm a big girl." I enjoyed being cradled in his arms.

Tenderly, he took my hand in his and stroked the side near the bandages. "Keep arguing and I'm going to spank you tonight."

"Oh," I whispered, butterflies filling my insides.

The vibrations of his deep laugh ricocheted through my body. "Maybe you'd like that."

"Morgan..." I relaxed into him.

"Listen, someone is after you. They came to my work and slashed my tires. I don't want to find you the same way we found Elvira. So you can't get rid of me, no matter how mouthy you are."

"Don't be silly," I said, feeling butterflies starting to float around my stomach. "You don't think someone would do that. Do you?" My heart quickened, beating feverishly inside my chest.

"I don't know, Race." His fingers trailed up my arm, running over my highly sensitive skin. "I won't take the chance."

"Okay" left my mouth a little too quickly.

I couldn't deny it any longer—at least, not to myself anymore.

Morgan DeLuca stirred all kinds of feelings inside of me.

I lusted after him.

That word might not even be enough to describe how badly I wanted him.

The moment his lips had touched mine, I had known I was a goner.

Never in my entire life had a man kissed me the way he had, let alone the way he fucked me.

"Good," he said against my hair as he traced tiny circles on my shoulder.

I sat there like a doe-eyed girl, basking in the feel of his skin against mine. "Morgan," I whispered, biting on my lip.

"Yeah?" His mouth brushed against my ear.

I shuddered. "This."

He held me tighter, resting his lips against my neck. "Listen, have you ever wanted something so badly that you never thought you'd want in a million years?"

I swallowed hard and nodded.

"I never thought I'd want to be with someone, Race. But then your bossy ass sat there on a barstool slinging all types of bullshit at me and everything inside me changed."

"You really like me?" I blinked.

Oh my God.

"Yes," he answered in a serious tone.

I stared straight ahead, not daring to make eye contact. "We don't really make sense."

"Let's take it one day at a time. I like you though. More than I ever expected or wanted to."

"I know. Me too." My cheeks heated.

He leaned forward and placed his mouth over mine. My breath was lost as he stole every bit of air inside my body, causing me to feel lightheaded and dizzy.

As his lips lingered over mine, he asked, "Do you want me in your bed?"

My mind was still hazy from the lust that had flooded my every fiber. "Yes."

Before I could take it back, he covered my mouth in another kiss.

A moment later, he backed away, holding me at arm's length. "I need you, Race, but not here," he said as his chest heaved. He tried to catch his breath, just as affected by the kiss as I had been.

"Johnny should be here soon," I said, unsure of what else to say.

"When he's done, I'll take you to dinner and then we can head home."

"What if I don't want to go home?"

"Then I'll take you anywhere you want, but eventually we'll end up at your place."

"And then?"

"Then we'll finish what we started."

Hope bloomed inside me, and self-doubt evaporated. Want flooded my system as I took in the man before me.

CHAPTER TWENTY

MORGAN

Beg For It

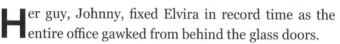

Her guy, Johnny, fixed Elvira in record time as the entire office gawked from behind the glass doors.

I graciously let Race drive Elvira as we headed to dinner.

Once we'd arrived at the restaurant, conversation was almost nonexistent for the first half of the meal. After she'd consumed three glasses of wine, she started to talk.

"Thanks for letting me drive your girl." She sloshed the wine around in her glass. "I really am sorry it happened because of me."

"Don't apologize any more." I wiped my mouth and tossed my napkin on the table. "It's in the past."

"Kind of like I'll be," she whispered.

"What?" I cocked my head.

"Nothing." She watched the liquid as it moved around, and her eyes became glassy. "Can I drive her home?"

"Let's get a few things clear. Shall we?" I asked, rubbing my hands against my pants. "I had a simple life. Then this blond-haired woman walked into my world with her attitude, sassy mouth, and killer body and wrecked everything."

"Well, I—"

"Every time I look into her emerald-green eyes, I feel myself falling deeper, losing a bit of my heart with each kiss. I've never felt like this before. I don't know how to act half the time. So don't toss aside my feelings for you. When your case is over, I'm far from done with you, Race True."

She sat there with her lips parted as she stroked her cleavage. "Okay." A small smile crept across her face. "Can I have more wine?"

"I want you fully lucid when I have you tonight. You'll beg for more."

"I've never begged, Morgan."

"You will tonight." I smirked.

Her throat moved as she swallowed hard and her lips parted wider. As her eyes softened, she uncrossed her arms and leaned forward.

"I don't fucking beg."

I scooted forward in my chair, moving my face as close as possible to hers. Our mouths were almost touching as her warm, wine-laden breath trailed across my lips. "You will for me tonight. That I promise you."

"Put up or shut up." The corner of her mouth twitched.

I grabbed my wallet, pulled out enough cash to more than cover the bill and tip, and stood. Holding my hand out, I stared down at her, ready to get out of there. "Let's see if you're all talk, princess."

"You're going to be the one walking funny tomorrow, big boy."

"I welcome the challenge."

"Let's watch a movie or something," I told her as we walked into her house.

She gawked at me. "Really?"

"No. Get your fine ass over here and kiss me, princess." I pointed to the floor near my feet.

"No foreplay?" She took one step forward.

"Oh, there'll be lots of that."

"No romance?"

"Dinner was the romance, and now, it's time for dessert."

"Are you sure you want to do this?" She glanced up at me from under her eyelashes.

"Do you want me?" I asked, crooking my finger at her, beckoning her forward.

"Uh, yeah."

"Or do you only want my enormous dick?" I teased, trying to lighten the mood.

"Well. I do want you, but you're not who I thought, Morgan." She took another step closer.

I leaned forward, bringing my lips close to hers. "Then kiss me, Race," I whispered, holding her chin in my hand.

Her eyes changed as I stared into them. She hesitated for a moment before her lips touched mine, hesitantly at first before her breathing changed and the kiss became more ravenous.

She wove her fingers through my hair, pulling me closer. Using both of my hands, I squeezed her ass, grinding against her. Her moans spilled into my mouth, making my cock even harder.

Leaving one hand on her ass, I fisted her hair in the other and pulled her mouth away from mine. As her head tipped back, I took the opportunity to taste her neck.

Her smooth skin smelled like sweet caramel as my tongue slid down the side of her neck. Taking my time, I explored her neck, stopping for a moment over her pulse. Her heart drummed against my lips in an erratic rhythm.

As my lips found the top of her breast, her fingernails dug into my forearms, piercing the skin. I hissed, sucking in a quick breath as my tongue darted out and slid against her silky tit.

"Don't stop," she cried out.

I'd come this far and there was nothing that would stop me now. After releasing her, I grabbed the bottom of her tank top and pulled it over her head. The delicate lace of her bra barely hid her breasts as her nipples strained against the material, yearning to be touched. I brushed the pad of my thumb against it, seeing her shudder.

Before I dropped to my knees, I unfastened her bra and tossed it to the floor. Touching the small of her back, I pulled her toward me and buried my face between her breasts. At that very moment, I wished I had more than one mouth. There wasn't a spot on her body I didn't want to devour, and patience wasn't something I had to spare.

My mouth went right and a hand cupped the left, making sure each would receive equal attention. Her hands dropped to her sides as she swayed. Her nipples grew even more taut as I sucked, and my cock strained for freedom.

When her body swayed again, I wrapped my arm around her back and held her steady. I alternated between each breast, using my teeth to give her a jolt when her body began to shake. I moaned, using the vibration to my advantage.

"You're killing me," she whined as I was about to switch sides again.

I didn't reply. Some situations didn't require words. I grazed her nipple with my teeth and undid the button on her jeans.

She wiggled as I pulled them down her legs. The girl had gone commando, and it was sexy as hell. All day she'd sat next to me with nothing between her pussy and me except for one scrap of material.

My fingers slid down her smooth mound and cupped her sex. I had to take a moment to regain my composure before I slid my fingers through her wetness. My mouth watered as the scent of her arousal finally hit me.

I groaned as I touched her pussy. Using the wetness on my fingers, I circled her clit, feeling the hardness against my fingertips. There was nothing I wanted to do more than to plunge my fingers inside her, but I wanted to tease her and make her beg for it.

I hadn't released her nipple, so I sucked on it harder as I circled her clit. Her body shook in my arms as she gripped my shoulders with shaky fingers.

"More," she moaned, pushing her pussy against my hand.

The wetness dripped from my fingers, coating them thoroughly as I prodded her opening. The last thing I wanted to do was hurt her, but I couldn't waste any more time. I needed to be inside her. It had taken everything in me to show the restraint I already had, and I wouldn't be able to hold out much longer.

Slowly, I sank one finger inside her, feeling her walls convulse around me. Touching her from the inside was almost heavenly. The only thing better would have been my dick, but there would be time for that.

"More," she called out.

Without releasing her nipple, I did as I'd been told. Dipping a second finger inside, I resisted the urge to cry out myself. My eyes rolled back in my head as the feeling of ecstasy overcame me.

I would not come in my pants. I couldn't. All credibility I had with Race would quickly go out the window. I left my fingers inside, not moving as I calmed myself down.

"More!"

She was a greedy little thing. I loved that. I wanted her to be aggressive.

"Harder."

It almost sounded like she was begging, although she'd argue that point. I did as she'd commanded, slowly moving my fingers out before plunging them back inside.

I needed to taste her.

As I worked my fingers inside her, I trailed a path down her stomach. Then I hovered just in front of her pussy. I paused, letting her musky female arousal penetrate every fiber of my being before I leaned forward and licked her.

"Fuck," she groaned, almost collapsing in my arms.

The salty sweetness of her exploded in my mouth. I swear to fuck, my dick was about to break off, and I was hanging by a thread as I fastened my mouth around her and captured her wetness with my tongue.

As I glanced up at her, her eyes rolled back and closed. I wouldn't let her come—not yet, at least. She'd have to beg for it. From the sounds coming from her throat, I knew I was on the right track, so I pushed forward and increased the pressure of my mouth against her bare flesh.

Just as her body began to shake and her breathing came out in ragged, short breaths, I pulled away.

"Don't stop."

"Beg," I demanded, still working my fingers inside her.

"Morgan," she said.

I ignored her, continuing my assault on her from the inside. After finding her G-spot, I let my fingers slide against it each time my digits retreated.

"Oh my God," she cried out, pushing her pussy toward my face. "You can't!"

"I can. God won't help you now. Only I can. Say it."

"Fuck you." Her fingers dug into my scalp, pulling my hair.

"You will."

She glared at me, still grinding against my hand. Her nipples were hard peaks and her skin was covered in goose bumps. "I hate you."

I stuck my tongue out and swept it across her clit, curling it to get maximum contact.

"Yes!"

I pulled away. "Yes what?" I hooked my fingers inside her so she couldn't move.

"Fuckin' eat me, Morgan."

Now that was sexy, but it wasn't enough. I slid a third finger inside, stretching her wide.

"Oh," she groaned. This time, her knees were weak enough that I held her up. If I moved, she'd fall back.

Her pussy clamped down. "Please, Morgan."

"Please, Morgan what?"

Now, I was just toying with her and being a total prick. I knew it, and I was sure she did too.

"Please let me come," she whispered, looking down at me with a softened face.

They all became sweet little things when their orgasms rested on their actions. If it weren't for my fingers inside her, I was sure she'd claw my eyeballs out.

Since she'd asked so nicely, I placed my mouth over her and toyed with her clit, applying just enough pressure to bring her close but nothing more.

She rose up on her tiptoes, trying to get closer to my face. I didn't protest, moving forward and burying my face in her flesh. Even if I suffocated, it would be one hell of a way to go.

Just as my jaw started to ache, her body trembled and her pussy contracted around my fingers. As she cried out my name, I increased the pressure of my mouth against her and thrust my fingers deeper inside her.

Her fingers pulled at my hair as she screamed, "Yes!"

By the time her body stopped twitching, my cock was about to explode. I could feel the blue balls slowly killing my member. I eased my fingers out, ready to get mine before there was nothing to be gotten.

I licked her off my fingers as I stood. Her eyes fluttered open and tried to focus on me. My need overcame my sensibilities as I undid my pants, leaving the zipper hanging open.

"Down you go." I pushed on her shoulders.

"Wait. What?" she asked as her knees bent from the pressure.

"I want to feel your mouth on me. Be a good girl and wrap your lips around my dick."

"Are you going to beg too?" She smirked as she slid the jeans down my legs.

"Please suck my cock, princess," I whispered as my dick sprang free and bobbed. My dick waved in her face as if taunting her.

She palmed it without hesitation, causing my junk to lurch forward. The silky warmth of her hands had me on the brink.

I needed to think about something other than my dick. I didn't want it to be over before it had even begun. As her tongue poked out, grabbing the wetness that had seeped from the tip, I almost had a heart attack.

The only thing I could think of to keep my mind off her was work. As the tip of my dick passed her lips, I wondered what the guys had done to secure backup for tomorrow night. I mentally rattled off a list of things I needed to speak to the guys about before the drop occurred.

Trying to keep my mind occupied didn't help for too long. Quickly, I ran out of shit to think about and could only feel her tongue stroking the underside of my shaft. Every time the tip of her tongue caressed the sensitive spot where the head met the stem, I shuddered.

It was my turn for my knees to feel weak. Her mouth demanded my attention as she took me deep, but not enough to swallow me whole. I couldn't take it any longer. I wanted to come. The last thing I cared about when I had my dick in her mouth was that I'd look weak if I came too quickly. I wasn't about to torture myself. We had all night, and this was just the appetizer.

"Put your hands on your knees," I commanded as I looked down.

If I were any bigger, I wouldn't have fit. There's nothing like seeing your cock buried inside a woman's mouth.

She swallowed against my cock as her hands fell to her legs and she looked at me with questioning eyes.

"You good?" I asked even though, no matter the answer, I was still going to do the same thing.

She gave a slight nod as drool started to pool at the corners of her lips.

I slid my hands down her hair and grasped it tightly in my fingers. I pushed my cock forward, slipping it down her throat just a little farther than it had been before. She gagged a little as her eyes closed. Her throat clamped down as she tried to swallow, and I almost erupted in her mouth.

When my tip bent slightly, curving down her throat, it was the most amazing feeling in the world, and I wasn't about to stop.

"Fuck, that feels so good," I murmured as I fucked her face.

She just stared up at me through teary eyes. Her tongue tried to keep up, pushing on the underside of my dick, but it wasn't necessary.

"I'm so close."

Instantly, she stopped fighting it, letting me take control of her body. Having Race on her knees, with my dick in her mouth and listening to my commands, was more than I could take. I exploded inside her.

Everything in the room went blurry. Come chills racked my body as my legs began to buckle. I gripped her hair tighter, grounding myself to her as support as I rode the wave of ecstasy.

By the time my orgasm had passed, I was breathless and panting. I couldn't get air in fast enough as I released her hair and leaned forward, completely winded.

"Jesus." I eased my softening cock from her mouth.

She wiped the corners of her mouth, pulling the last drops of me onto her tongue before swallowing.

If my dick were hard, I would've come again from seeing her do that.

"Good girl." I stroked the side of her cheek, finding a little bit she'd missed.

I placed the pad of my thumb against her mouth. "Open up. One last drop."

As I slid my finger inside, my dick twitched but quickly fell flat, totally milked and spent.

"I can't decide if you're an asshole or not," she muttered after she'd swallowed.

"But you like me anyway."

"Hardly," she shot back as she climbed to her feet.

"Your pussy says otherwise."

"Bastard."

"I bet you're still wet. Maybe wetter after sucking my cock." I grabbed her arms and pulled her toward me.

"Am not." She pushed against my chest.

Reaching down, I slid my fingers through her, feeling her wetter than before. She moaned as her mouth fell open and then she gasped. After raking her with my fingertips, I brought them back up to our faces.

"Liar," I murmured as I placed them against my tongue and brought her mouth to mine. I wanted her to taste exactly what I had—her on my tongue.

I wasn't done with her yet.

The night was still young.

CHAPTER TWENTY-ONE

RACE

Try Me, Princess

I twirled my finger against his pec, making tiny circles. "You don't understand how I grew up."

As he stroked the side of my arm, he inched his body closer, resting his chin on top of my head. "Tell me, then."

"It's so boring."

"I don't think anything you say is boring."

"Fine," I whispered as I caressed his skin. "My mother was a total religious prude."

"Was?" He squeezed my shoulder.

"She's alive. Don't worry. We haven't spoken in years though."

"I'm sorry."

"I'm not. She was a nightmare after my father died. She had always been religious, but after he passed, she became a fanatic."

"She's one of those people. Sorry, kid." He kissed my hair before adjusting our bodies. He slid downward, making us face each other.

Fucking hell.

It was easier to confess stuff to him when I didn't have to look him in the eyes.

"She was ashamed of me. I could never do anything right in her eyes anymore. Every day, she'd tell me I was going to hell for something or other. I had enough of it after I left for college. I haven't spoken to her since the day I stepped on campus."

He brushed his fingers against my cheek. "Do you regret it?" he asked as his face softened.

I shook my head. "Not at all. I'd rather be alone than listen to her tell me I'm not good enough every day."

"Is that why your work is so important to you?"

I nodded and wished it weren't true. "It's all I have. My family has fallen apart. Some of it is my fault, but I've committed myself to my work. I'm good at it, and I want to make a name for myself."

"You will." He touched me tenderly.

"If we get the tape back," I whispered.

"There's no we, and it'll all be over tomorrow," he said. "About that." He removed his hand from my face.

"What?" My stomach dropped.

"I found a current connection between you and Tyler O'Shea."

"Oh my God, tell me."

"His wife works at your company." He winced after he spoke. "I'm sorry I didn't tell you sooner."

"Who is she?" I demanded, now going through everyone I knew from work. "I don't know anyone with the last name O'Shea."

"She never took his name when they married. I found it when I was searching through his records."

"Fuck." I grabbed my cheeks and dragged my hands down my face. "Are you going to tell me who it is?"

"Nope." He shook his head.

I glared at him. "Why the fuck not?"

"Race," he said in a soft tone, scooting forward in the bed, "I will not allow you to put yourself in danger. If I tell you who she is, you'll go after her."

"I would not. And what's with the 'you won't allow me' bullshit?" I asked, feeling my jaw tense. Who in the fuck did this man think he was?

"You hired me to do a job, and I'm going to do it."

"You're fired."

"No, I'm not," he said. "Remember, I'll tie you up before I let you put yourself at risk."

I crossed my arms over my chest. "You wouldn't."

"Try me, princess." He smirked.

I gnawed on the inside of my lip, debating my next words. "Can I help, at least?"

"No. Absolutely not."

My shoulders sagged. "But if I don't go, I'll never get the tape back." I toyed with the sheet near my feet and refused to look at him.

"Hey." He touched my chin.

"What?" I asked, trying to figure out how to get the tape back myself.

"Remember when you said you trusted me?"

"Yes," I mumbled, staring at his lips.

"You have to trust me now, Race." He brought my eyes to his.

"I do, but so much can go wrong."

"Nothing will go wrong. You have an entire team of men behind you."

"Do they have an opening for a businesswoman? Because when that tape gets released, I'll be blackballed."

"You're so dramatic." He rolled his eyes.

I straightened my back, squaring my shoulders. "Since I'm the one paying, I should be able to help out in any way I see fit,"

"Baby," he murmured as he leaned forward to kiss me.

I weaved, avoiding the contact. "Don't 'baby' me."

He hovered over my lips, staring me straight in the eyes. "I'll talk to the guys and ask them if they think it's okay. All right?"

I glared at him, knowing he was just pacifying me. "Fine." I was going to find a way to be there when the shit went down.

I didn't have a choice. It was my life hanging in the balance, and no one would look out for me like I would.

No one.

I was the only person I could rely on in my life. It was how it'd been for years. I was okay with it. I had grown used to it. I couldn't just hand my future over to a man. That was how I'd gotten into this mess to begin with.

My father had taught me to trust my instincts.

CHAPTER TWENTY-TWO

MORGAN

Don't Let Her Run

Race's eyes grew wide, her mouth hanging open as I walked into her office. "What are you doing here?"

"Hey, princess." I took in the majesty of her office. I was totally impressed by the size. "I thought I'd drop by and see how things were going."

She glanced at her watch before glaring at me. "It's almost five. Aren't you supposed to be getting ready to go meet *him*?"

I nodded, tapping on my watch. "Plenty of time."

She sighed, pushing herself away from her desk before stalking toward me. "No, there isn't."

"Everything is set. We're just waiting for seven to roll around. The day is dragging. I thought stopping by would be a great way to pass the time."

She slid her hand up my arm and rested it on my shoulder. "Did you talk to the guys about me tagging along tonight?"

"Yeah. They said that you can meet us at six thirty at the office and we'll head out from there." I was fucking lying through my teeth.

Her eyebrows shot up. "Really?"

"Yeah," I lied again. I was going to have to do some major groveling later to make up for the bullshit falling out of my mouth.

"Thank you." She leaned forward and gave me a kiss square on the lips.

As she started to pull away, I wrapped my arms around her waist and brought her body flush with mine.

"Where are you going? I need more of that," I murmured against her lips.

"Morgan." She pushed against my chest. "I can't get caught here at work."

"Doesn't everyone knock?" I peered over her shoulder toward the door.

"Yeah, but—"

I cut her off, covering her mouth with mine and breathing her in.

She moaned into my mouth as she pulled the breath from my lungs. I pulled her tighter against me, wrapping her in my arms.

What the fuck was I doing?

I hadn't gone there to fuck her, let alone kiss her. I wanted to drop by, say hello, have a quick chat with Natasha, and then make sure Race wouldn't make the seven o'clock meeting tonight. But here I was, in a lip-lock with Race.

I broke the kiss. "I gotta stop."

"What if I don't want you to?" she asked with lipstick-smudged lips, panting.

"I just wanted to drop by and see how you were and tell you about tonight." I licked my lips, savoring every drop of her left behind.

"That's all you wanted?" She backed away as she adjusted her shirt.

"Yep. That's all," I lied.

Three times I'd lied to her face. She'd probably have me by the balls later for it, but it was the right thing to do.

"Ms. True," her secretary called through the door as she knocked.

"Fix your lips," I whispered, touching my mouth.

"Shit," she muttered, running to her desk. She grabbed a mirror and tried to fix her lipstick but failed. "Yes?"

Her secretary walked in, glancing between us as she walked toward Race's desk. She gave me a quick wink before turning her full attention to her boss. "Natasha wanted to go over the notes for your meeting tomorrow before she leaves tonight. She asked me to give them to you and to have you phone her when you're ready."

Natasha. That was Tyler's wife—and possibly an accomplice in his scheme to ruin Race's career. I hadn't told her about Natasha yet, and I still didn't feel the time was right, but I had to warn her.

Race took the notes from the woman and flipped through the pages. "I'll give them a quick read, Cara. Call her and tell her to come to my office in five."

The woman nodded and turned on her heel to face me. "Are you sure you'll be done?" Cara asked as her eyes raked over me from head to toe, and with a grin so dirty, I knew exactly what she had on her mind.

"Yes. We're done here. Mr. DeLuca was on his way out."

"Shame," Cara whispered before she sauntered toward the door and left.

Race looked up from her notes with her eyebrows knitted together. "What did she say?"

"Nothing." I shrugged.

She tossed the papers on the desk and collapsed in her chair. "Is there anything else you need, Morgan?"

"Oh, we're back to Morgan?"

"Stop." She rubbed her forehead. "I have to finish my work so I can be out of here on time tonight. There's no way I'm going to miss it."

"But it's okay if you can't make it tonight. I'd prefer it if you weren't there." It was the only truthful thing I'd said since I'd walked through her office door.

"I'm going. Don't even try to talk me out of it. Now go so I'm not late."

I waved. "Yes, ma'am," I said before I left.

As the door clicked closed, a loud bang made me jump.

"What the hell?" I asked as I turned around.

Cara walked over to me, touching my arm. More like she groped my arm as she stared up at me. "Don't mind her. Oh, you must work out." She squeezed my forearms, working her way up to just above my elbows.

"Cara..."

"I'm too old for you, Mr. DeLuca. I'm just wondering what your intentions are toward Ms. True."

"Um, I don't know."

"Honey, the woman needs a man. I saw the look on her face when I walked in the room. I saw her bee-stung lips and red lipstick still smeared on her face. I think you're just what the doctor ordered. Just perfect."

"Thanks." I laughed. "I'm trying my best."

"The woman works too much. Life's too short and she's too young to always spend it in the office. Just treat her right, Mr. DeLuca."

"Morgan," I corrected her.

"Morgan," she repeated, dropping her hand from my arm.

The sound of a person clearing their throat made us both turn.

"Am I interrupting?" the woman asked, glaring at me and giving us both a look of disgust.

Cara shook her head as she sat down and started moving papers around on the desk. "I was just saying goodbye, ma'am. You're a few minutes early, but I'm sure Ms. True is ready for you."

In front of me stood Natasha.

The vibe she threw off was that of a megabitch.

Although Race carried herself with authority, she had nothing on Natasha. Her pin-straight black hair was pulled up in a bun so tight that I wondered if it altered the look of her face. Her business suit was perfect, not a wrinkle on it, as if she'd stood all day to avoid any imperfections.

"And you are?" Natasha asked in a snotty tone as she looked me over, but not like Cara had before. Natasha looked at me like a low-class citizen who wasn't fit to breathe the same air she was breathing.

"Mr. DeLuca," I replied as I looked at her the exact same way she had me, but I held my hand out, trying to be courteous.

She glanced down and snarled. "I'm sure she's ready for me," Natasha said as she walked past me and entered Race's office without knocking.

"Wow," I muttered to myself before the door closed.

"She's a real treat," Cara said before sticking her finger in her mouth. "She's one of the ugliest people I know."

I wondered if Cara was the eyes and ears in this place. Typically, secretaries talked. If there was a bitchy boss,

I wondered how much information was shared between them.

"Let me ask you something," I whispered as I leaned on Cara's desk to be close enough not to be overheard.

"Anything you want, handsome." She gazed up at me.

"Natasha. Good person or bad? I think I know the answer."

"Nothing but bad there."

"How bad?" I rubbed my chin.

"She'd sell her own mother for personal gain. She's the worst there is here. No one likes her, and poor Ms. True has to work with her. They're both in line for partnership. It's dog-eat-dog, and I worry Natasha will do anything to win."

"I'll make sure that doesn't happen," I said even though I didn't know how in the fuck I'd do that. But I knew that if Natasha were involved, I wouldn't let her destroy Race.

"Who are you, Morgan?" She rested her chin in her palm, giving me dreamy eyes.

"I may be done before anything gets started."

"Well, isn't that confusing?"

"If you see me again, I'll answer it. Right now, everything is in the air."

"Don't let her run," she whispered. "She needs a tight leash, that one." Cara covered her mouth. "Don't ever tell her I said that."

I ran my fingers across my lips and replied, "My lips are sealed."

"Cara!" a voice yelled from the other side of the closed door.

She pushed back from the desk. "You better go before we get ourselves in trouble."

I nodded. I liked Cara. I felt like we could be good friends. "I'm out. Nice chatting with you, Cara."

"Any time, handsome. Come back, ya hear?" She waved before disappearing into Race's office.

As soon as I exited the building, I dialed Johnny. "Hey, this is Race's friend from the other day."

"Hi, son. What can I do for you?"

"Race is going to call you tonight. I need a favor."

"Anything you or Race need, I'm there for you."

"Here's what I need you to do for me," I said before setting my plan into motion.

CHAPTER TWENTY-THREE

RACE

I'm Coming, STFU

After I changed into a pair of black track pants, a formfitting, black tank top, and matching sneakers, I headed for the door. I probably looked like a complete fool, but I couldn't exactly show up in my business suit.

For once, I got out of the office on time.

I walked toward my car, feeling the summer sun beating down against my clothing as it scorched my skin underneath.

Me: I'm on my way.

I texted Morgan before I rifled through my purse to grab my keys. As I approached my car, I could see immediately that something was wrong.

I closed my eyes, drawing deep breaths through my nose.

This can't be happening. No. No.

This can't be happening.

One of my tires was flat. I wasn't going anywhere any time soon.

"Fuck." I gripped my keys hard enough that they dug into the cuts on my hands, making me wince.

"Motherfucker!" I yelled out, trying to steady my breathing but finding it impossible.

I closed my eyes again. Tears started to form as I stood there, trying not to be hysterical.

Just as I was about to throw my shit everywhere in a mini fit, my phone beeped.

Morgan: When will you be here?

I replied through watery eyes, having to erase my message a few times before getting it right.

Me: As soon as I can get a cab. I have a flat tire.
Morgan: Do not leave the office.

He can't be serious.

I didn't care if I had to walk to the damn meeting spot; I was going to be there. I tried to hold the phone steady as I typed back with shaky fingers.

Me: I'm coming. STFU.

I tossed my keys in my purse, giving my car one more look before marching back toward the office building. I stopped three steps away from the front door, dialing Johnny.

He answered the phone with his same old greeting. "Johnny's Auto."

"Hey, Johnny. It's Race."

"Baby girl, twice in one week. I couldn't be so lucky."

A pang of guilt sliced through me. He seemed to like talking about my father as much as I did, and he was the only connection I had to talk with about him now.

"I'm sorry, Johnny. I should call you more."

"I know you're busy, kid. You're a high-powered businesswoman now. Your daddy would've been so proud."

"I need your help." I avoided his statement about my father. I didn't want to lose time by chatting about the olden days. There would be time for that later, but Tyler needed to be dealt with today.

"What can I do for ya?"

"I have a flat tire. I need your help, Johnny."

"Seems to be common problem this week."

"Yeah." I laughed through my tears. "Can you help me?"

"I can. I'll be there as soon as possible."

"Johnny," I said, twirling the keys on my index finger as I started through the door of the office building, "I won't be here when you get here. I'll leave the keys with security."

"Where are you going?" he asked, panic evident in his voice.

I stopped mid-step. "What does it matter?"

"It doesn't. I just don't know which car is yours."

It couldn't be true.

Did Morgan do this?

He couldn't have.

He wouldn't have.

He said I could go.

But he didn't want me to go.

Who the hell was I kidding?

Even if he had forbidden it, I would find a way to be there.

"Johnny, did Morgan call you today?" I narrowed my eyes as my nostrils flared.

"Well, um. No," he whispered.

"Fuck. Seriously. You're both working against me."

"No!" Johnny yelled. "Race, he just doesn't want you to get hurt. I don't know what kind of trouble you're in."

"Stop."

"But—"

"Johnny, I'm a grown woman. I've always dealt with my problems, and I'll do it again. No one is ever going to tell me no. Keys are with the security guard. I'll text you the address, and I drive a BMW Alpina B6. It'll be the one with the flat tire."

"Race, I don't think you should—"

I didn't hear the rest of his statement. I hit end on the screen, hanging up on Johnny.

Morgan's a fucking asshole.

I should've known he'd pull some shit to make sure I couldn't be there. I knew I could never trust a man. They all thought they knew what was best.

I only had one thing to do. I'd call a cab and go directly to the meeting location. Fuck them all. I'd get my tape back myself and show the guys that I didn't need them after all.

After I'd left my keys with security, I went outside to wait for the taxi. I paced, becoming more pissed with each passing second.

Morgan DeLuca was going to pay—right after I helped to bring Tyler O'Shea down and retrieved my video.

I had my best friend in my purse, my Beretta PX4.

Tyler would give me that video.

Anything to save my career.

I'd have to deal with Morgan another day.

He'd wish he'd never met me by the time I was done with him.

Just as I tossed the gun back in my purse, the taxi pulled in.

It was now or never.

CHAPTER TWENTY-FOUR

MORGAN

Hell to Pay

"**D**ude, that takes balls," Sam said as he drove to the abandoned warehouse.

Race was far from stupid. She'd figure it out sooner or later, and it wouldn't be a pretty sight when she saw me again.

> **Race: As soon as I can get a cab. I have a flat tire.**

"I'll pay for it later." I stared out the passenger window with a knot in my stomach.

"If there is a later." Thomas slapped me on the back of the head.

"What's that supposed to mean?" I ignored the fact that he'd hit me and replied to her text.

> **Me: Do not leave the office.**

"She'll probably never talk to you again, man." Thomas shook his head. "You lied to her. Never mind about the tire."

"Yep. You're never getting another shot with her," James added. "Izzy would murder me."

"Race will get over it," I said, shrugging it off.

"I doubt that. I've only met her a couple of times, but she doesn't seem like the type to forgive and forget," Thomas said.

"I'm not saying I won't pay dearly for it, guys, but I think I can handle her." I glanced in the backseat.

"You like this girl that much, huh?" James asked.

"I don't know why, but I do. God help me." I looked up at the roof and blew out a long breath.

"It's the magic of the tough chick," James replied as he patted my shoulder. "I know it well."

"I just can't picture my cousin dealing with your bullshit."

"My bullshit?" He snickered, clutching his chest. "Have you met your cousin? That girl has more tricks up her sleeve than Houdini."

"How do you deal with her?"

"You gotta break her."

"What?" I turned around with my mouth agape.

"James." Thomas glared at him. "You're talking about my sister here. Choose your next words *very* carefully."

James slapped Thomas on the leg. "No worries, brother." He glanced at me, lifting his chin in my direction. "We'll talk about the ladies later, Morgan."

I returned his chin lift. "I'll take you up on that offer."

"Five minutes out," Sam said. "We ready for this?" He adjusted his body, gripping the steering wheel so hard that his knuckles had turned white.

"You okay, man?" I asked Sam, placing my hand on his shoulder.

"I'm pumped. I've been on the sidelines for a bit. I'm so excited. This shit is like the olden days."

"The olden days sucked," James said, hanging his head.

"Oh, stop with your Debbie Downer shit, James," Thomas barked. "Everyone knows the plan, yeah?"

"Why don't you go over it again, because clearly we may have missed something the ten times you've already reviewed it with us," James teased.

The final minutes of the car ride were in silence. Each of us checked our equipment, removed safeties, and got mentally focused. Sam had secured permission from the owner of the next building to stash the car inside to avoid being spotted by Tyler.

After the car was hidden, we all took our positions and waited. Sam took the roof, being our lookout, while James, Thomas, and I took our spots around the building.

I was so nervous that I could barely focus. My heart was pounding in my throat and my palms felt slick from the nonstop perspiration that formed every time I wiped them on my jeans.

If this shit didn't go down right, her life could be in a shambles and it would be entirely my fault.

I couldn't let her take a chance with her life. She might be an adult, but like hell would I let her walk into a fire when I could put it out without her getting involved.

I glanced at my watch and realized more than ten minutes had passed while I'd been standing here. Tyler hadn't arrived.

"He's late," James said in my earpiece, figuring out the same thing I had.

"Let's wait ten more minutes before we call it," Thomas replied.

"I don't see anyone coming either," Sam added.

"Fuck," I said as my stomach began to sink. "I bet the fucker doesn't show." I had a feeling I couldn't explain. I'd felt it once or twice in the army, and typically shit went bad.

"What do we want to do?" James's voice echoed in my ear.

"I think you're right, Morgan. We'll wait five and leave," Thomas replied.

I crouched down, picked up tiny pebbles, and tossed them. My mind was racing, and just standing here was making me crazy. I didn't like the unknown.

I pulled my phone from my pocket, needing to check on Race.

Me: Sorry we left without you. No time to spare.

"Men, I think it's time to pack it in," Thomas said.

"Did you hear from Angel? Race said she was going to head to the office," I said, heading toward the building we'd hid the vehicle in.

"Meet at the truck. I'll call Angel on the way," Thomas replied.

"Ten-four," James said. "Something's off for sure."

"What are you thinking?" Sam asked over the radio.

"I don't know, but I know something bad is happening."

"Thomas, call Angel," I demanded as sweat lined my brow.

"I'm doing it, fucker."

Before I'd made it to the van, he said the words I didn't want to hear.

"She never made it, man."

Bile rose in my throat and I tried my best to swallow it down. "Everyone, get your ass back here."

"What are you thinking, Morgan?" James appeared at my side.

"I don't know, man, but I think we definitely got played. There is no way in hell anything would stop Race from showing up here today. I may have told her not to, but I knew she wouldn't listen." I tried to keep calm, but on the inside, I was crumbling.

"We'll find her, man." James patted me on the shoulder. "Move your asses," he barked into the radio.

"Fuck me." I shrugged his hand away. "I did this."

"Stop being a pussy," James blurted. "You didn't do shit."

I started to hyperventilate. "I did." I drew in a shaky breath, pushing down the fear that started to grip me. "If she were here, I'd know she was safe."

"Yo!" Sam yelled as he jogged into the building, Thomas right on his heels.

"We're all here. Move your asses," Thomas said, pointing toward the truck.

I pushed the fear away, readying myself for battle.

I'd get her back.

I climbed into the car, feeling on edge but ready to kick Tyler's ass.

Who was I kidding?

I planned to wring his neck until I choked the very last breath out of him.

The car ride was a whirlwind.

Thomas and James were on the phone with contacts, gathering intel and trying to find someone willing to hack into the phone records to try to pinpoint her location. I tried to text her and call her again, but she didn't respond or pick up.

Even if she were livid with me, she would have texted me back. I'd made it pretty clear how worried I was and that she was in grave danger, but nada. No reply from Race.

"She isn't responding," I said after the fifth text.

"I got a guy working on her location." James flipped the phone in his hand.

"We're just about there," Sam called out, moving his face closer to the window, sitting forward and ready to go.

When James's phone rang, the car grew silent. "Hit me," James said as he stared at me.

Please let her be okay.

"Got it. On our way there now," James said before disconnecting the call. "Last known location was her office. After that, the signal goes cold. Someone turned her phone off."

"Motherfucker." I punched the dashboard.

"Stay calm, man." Thomas grabbed my shoulder.

"Easy for you to say." I closed my eyes as my chest tightened. "I need to find my woman."

"Listen, we've done this shit more than once. We always get the girl back. Always," Thomas said in a calm, even voice.

"It's almost an inauguration of sorts around these parts. Angel was kidnapped and Izzy was abducted. Somehow, they're still alive and breathing."

"What the fuck?" I jerked my head back. "What the hell did you guys get me involved in?"

"Life isn't always pretty," James replied, giving me a shrug.

"It happens when you live your life on the edge, Morgan. You wouldn't be so upset if you didn't have feelings for Race."

"Fuck you! I'd still be pissed off that we were duped," I shot back.

"Yeah, but it stings because you fucked up and you like the girl. I promise we'll get her back," Thomas said, staring out the window, surveying the parking lot as we pulled in.

Before the truck came to a stop, I opened my door and hopped out, using the extra speed to run toward the doors.

I could see Johnny's truck in the distance near Race's car. She'd called, just like I'd assumed, but where the fuck was she?

"James," I yelled, stopping near the entrance as the guys climbed out. "Go see if Race is over there by her car."

He nodded, jogging away quickly.

"Excuse me, sir?" I asked, trying to catch my breath as I ran inside.

"Yes?" the portly security guard asked as he rose from his chair.

"Did you see a blond woman leave here about thirty minutes ago?" I leaned on the desk, ready to push off and run.

"Do you mean Ms. True?" A smile spread across his face.

"Yes." My jaw stiffened.

"Why, yes. She was waiting outside for a taxi last I saw her," he replied.

"Did she get in a taxi?"

His lips bunched as his forehead drew down. "I don't know, sir. I didn't pay attention."

"Fucking great," I muttered, squeezing my eyes shut.

"Find her?" James asked as he jogged through the doors.

"She isn't here," I replied as I made tight fists, trying not to punch something.

"Not outside, either."

"Fucking hell. We lost her." I started to pace.

James touched my shoulder. "Come on, man. Let's go to the office. We'll find her."

"We better," I whispered.

I wasn't done with Race True.

This wasn't how we were supposed to end.

CHAPTER TWENTY-FIVE

RACE

Darkness

Darkness surrounded me.

I lay here frozen, unable to see, as my eyes were covered by something.

My bones ached, my head throbbed, and I couldn't move. My hands and feet were bound, my torso strapped down, leaving me unable to so much as wiggle.

What the fuck happened?

The only sounds in the room were my labored breathing and the sob that was about to burst from my throat.

It all came flooding back to me.

The flat tire.

Waiting outside for the taxi.

Tossing my gun in my purse.

And then... I gasped for air. Then the attack.

I hadn't seen it, but I'd felt the blow to my jaw as the pain radiated across my face. As I'd grabbed my chin, I was struck in the head. As the world had gone dim, my knees had crumpled and I'd fallen to the ground.

I had been so consumed by my anger toward Morgan that I hadn't been aware of my surroundings.

It was my fault I was here.

I began to cry.

"Hello?" I whispered so low that I barely heard it myself.

I held my breath, waiting for a reply, but heard nothing in response as tears streamed down my cheeks.

I need to take slow breaths and keep myself calm, I told myself over and over again.

I couldn't do it.

Who the fuck could keep their wits about them in a situation like this? Seriously. I'd like to think I was pretty levelheaded, but right now images of *Texas Chainsaw Massacre* kept playing over and over again inside my head.

Pulling at the restraints, I started to hyperventilate.

My heart beat so furiously that it was all I could hear.

A door opened, making me freeze.

"Ah, you're awake," said a woman from a distance.

I held my breath, waiting for my heart to explode as her heels clicked against the floor.

"Can you help me?" I whispered, remaining still.

She cackled, slapping the bottom of my feet. "Silly, Race."

I tried to flinch, but I couldn't move an inch. The tender flesh stung where her hand had landed.

"Please. I'll do anything you ask," I said, my voice strained.

"You know, you're not as light as you look." She dragged her fingernails up the side of my leg, leaving fire in their wake. "Always the perfect skinny bitch with perfect tits and never a bit out of place."

I gasped.

I knew the voice. The acidic tone was one I'd heard before.

Natasha.

The coworker I'd thought I was friends with.

She had to be Tyler's wife.

"Where's Tyler? Did he put you up to this?" I asked, trying to swallow but not finding enough moisture to make it possible.

"You think you have everything figured out, don't you?" she snarled in my ear, sending shivers down my spine. "Tyler was never behind this, darling."

Wait. What?

"You've been the one sending me messages?" My stomach turned.

"Your hired goons didn't figure it out, did they? They pegged my husband all along." She dragged her nails down my arm, pressing harder than she had on my leg.

The skin had started to break, but I bit my lip. "Let me go, please, Natasha." I tried not to scream.

"Don't be a silly girl, Race. I've got you right where I want you." Her heels tapped against the floor as she took three short steps away from me.

The sound of metal clinking in the background put my senses on high alert. "I'll do anything."

One step.

Two steps.

Three steps.

"You don't get it, do you?" she purred in my ear.

"Tell me. I'll make it right." I turned my head toward the sound of her voice, trying to see through the dark material covering my eyes, but I saw only darkness.

"There's nothing you can do," she said calmly.

"I thought we were friends." I fought back the tears I knew I couldn't wipe away.

Cold metal touched my cheek, the sharpness of the edge biting into my flesh. "We *were* friends."

I stilled.

"Until I found Tyler watching your video." Her warm breath skidded across my face. "I thought he loved me, but it was never me that he had been thinking about."

"But you're his wife." Nothing like stating the obvious to a crazy person as she held a knife against my face—no doubt I was thinking about as clearly as she was.

"I am, but you're the one he thinks about when he touches himself. Not me!" she yelled in my ear, making me flinch.

"But I—"

She pressed the blade deeper into my skin. "Keep your fucking mouth shut! Imagine how my heart shattered when I walked in on him. He sat there, moaning as he watched you on the screen and pictured you doing *those* things to him."

I gasped.

"It's you that he fantasizes about. You're the one he makes love to. I knew it, but I didn't believe it until he said your name in his sleep."

"Natasha, I never ever knew Tyler. I swear I had no idea." My breath caught as the blade slid under the blindfold.

Squinting, I tried to focus my eyes as the material fell to the table. I blinked, trying to clear the tears away.

Natasha stood above me, shifting with the blade in her grip. She snarled as the blade turned over in her hands.

"I'm going to make you pay for what you've done to me," she growled.

I pulled at the restraints. "I didn't do anything! Please just let me go." My lips trembled.

She shook her head as she ground her teeth, clenching her jaw tight.

I squeezed my eyes shut, bracing myself.

She leaned forward with the knife, cutting through the fabric of my tank with ease.

I gasped for air as my head spun.

Using the tip, she pushed the tattered shreds to the side, exposing my bra.

I tensed, giving a guttural scream with a closed mouth.

"I'm sure he loves these." She ran the blade across the tops of my breasts and my skin broke out into goose bumps.

"Please!" I shrieked, tensing my muscles. "Please don't do this."

She wagged the knife in front of my face, taunting me. "Are you scared, Race?" She smirked.

"Yes. I'll do anything. Please," I begged, shaking my head as she leaned forward with the blade.

I closed my eyes. I couldn't look. I held my breath as tears streamed down my face.

Blazing pain, unlike anything I'd ever felt before, sliced through my body so hard that I became winded. I screamed in pain, pulling at the restraints, tossing my head back and forth. "Stop, please!" I cried out, feeling dizzy.

I prayed to black out.

Begged for mercy, but nothing.

Just uncontrollable agony that radiated throughout my body.

When she lifted the knife, blood dripped from the edge, falling to my chest. Her eyes widened as her lips parted.

"You look better already." She walked around the table.

I tried to steady my breathing, focusing on something else other than the pain. I felt the blood as it oozed from the wound, traveling down my side and pooling underneath my back.

"No. I can't." I sucked in a breath, trying to grip the table and prepare myself for more torment. "Please don't do this," I cried as my body began to shake.

"Ah, pretty, Race. Are you worried you won't be perfect anymore?" she teased as the blade came down again.

As I cried and screamed, blackness took me.

CHAPTER TWENTY-SIX

MORGAN

Tyler Motherfuckin' O'Shea

I kicked the front door in, jerking my head until I found him. "Where the fuck is she?" I headed straight for him, lunging at him.

"What the fuck?" He put his hands up to cover his face.

"Don't play stupid. What the fuck did you do with her?" I wrapped my fingers around his neck, holding him against the wall.

His eyes bulged out as he gasped for air. "I don't know what you're talking about!"

"What do you mean you don't know what the fuck we're talking about?" I yelled, glaring at him.

He pulled at my fingers, trying to lessen the pressure around his neck. "I don't. I swear to God."

"Listen, motherfucker. I'll choke the last breath out of you right now," I growled. "Tell me where the fuck you're keeping Race."

"Race," he whispered, his eyes growing wider.

"Race. Where the fuck is she?" I squeezed tighter.

"Wait. I love Race." He dropped his hands to his sides.

"What?" My mouth fell open.

"I wouldn't hurt her. I love her," he babbled.

I lessened the pressure against his throat enough for him to speak, but not enough for him to get out of my hold.

"I wouldn't hurt her. I swear, man."

"Morgan!" Thomas yelled from behind me. "Let him go. He can't get away, and we can't get information if you kill him."

"Dude, fuckin' let him go." James patted my arm. "We won't let him get away."

"You should listen to your friends," Tyler said in a strangled voice.

I closed my eyes and applied just enough pressure to remind him that I held his fate in my hands. "If you fuckin' say one thing I don't like, I'll break your neck."

"Yes, sir," Tyler said, trying to nod under my fingertips.

I released him, pushing his body and slamming his head into the wall in the process. "You better start fuckin' talking."

Thomas and Sam stood at the foot of the steps with their guns out and ready to shoot, and James had my back.

Tyler reached for his throat. "Why do you think I have Race?" he asked as he rubbed his skin and swallowed.

"She got your messages about the video," I snarled as I stood one foot in front of him and didn't move.

"How do you know about the video?" he asked, his eyes as wide as saucers.

"Um, again, asshole. You sent her e-mails blackmailing her. I don't have time for this shit. Where the fuck is she?" I yelled, punching him in the stomach and watching him crumple.

He crouched over, holding his stomach. "I haven't told anyone about the video. It's still in my study."

"Someone knows. If you don't have Race, then who the fuck else could know about it?" James moved closer to Tyler.

"You got this all wrong. I'd never hurt her. I loved her from the moment I laid eyes on her in college. My lucky asshole cousin dated her. When he died, I found the tape, and I've never let it out of my sight."

"Sick bastard," Sam said.

"Who else fuckin' knows?" I pushed him back against the wall.

"Only Natasha. She kind of caught me once and..." He dragged his hands through his hair, still trying to catch his breath.

"Natasha. Where the hell is she?" I asked, looking around the room. "Sam, go look for her!" I yelled, holding Tyler in my grip.

Sam nodded and disappeared.

"She's not here, fucker," Tyler said. "She hasn't come home from work yet."

"Where's the video?"

"In my office," he said, pointing to his right.

"Show me." I turned him and pushed him down the stairs. "Try anything and Thomas there will put a bullet in your head."

"Jesus. I'm not stupid, man." He walked slowly with us inches behind.

As he approached his desk, I grabbed his arm and pulled him back. "Don't even think about it," I warned, increasing my hold.

"In the top drawer, in the back. Get it yourself." He glared at me.

"I'll get it," Thomas said. He pulled the drawer out, turned it over, and reached for a disc. "Got it." he shouted, putting it in his pocket.

"Where the hell would Natasha take Race?"

Tyler flinched. "I don't know."

"I don't have time for this shit." I pulled the gun from my holster and held it against his temple. "Where's Natasha?"

Tyler began to shake as he closed his eyes. "I don't know. Maybe the beach house," he offered as his lips began to tremble.

I lowered my gun. "You're coming with us, motherfucker." I pulled him forward, placing my weapon back in the holster.

"But why?"

"Because," James answered as we walked out of the office, "you know where the house is, and if she isn't there, we'll need you some more."

"Or I may kill you." I pulled him with me.

"Fuck," he muttered.

"Stop being an asshole." Thomas walked by us both and slapped Tyler in the head. "You're the reason Race is in this mess. You're sure as fuck going to help us get her out of it."

"Fine." Tyler straightened and walked of his own volition. "I don't want anything to happen to her."

"To your wife?" James asked with one eyebrow raised.

"No." Tyler snickered. "She's a coldhearted bitch. I meant Race."

"Sam." I ignored Tyler's statement about Race. "Let's go."

I'd never let Tyler near her again.

Whether he was involved in this shit or not, he would never, ever touch her.

Just as I stuffed Tyler in the backseat, Sam appeared in the doorway and headed straight for the car.

"If one hair on her head—" I started, but James stopped me with a hand on my shoulder.

"Stay calm. We need you calm, man. She needs you calm."

"I'm as calm as I'm going to get."

"We'll get her back," he said, but I knew they were empty words.

"Drive faster," I told Sam, feeling my very sanity start to slip.

"On it," he said, adjusting himself in the seat and stepping on the gas. "We're ten minutes out."

CHAPTER TWENTY-SEVEN

RACE

The End

"**R**ace," a voice whispered in my ear, but it sounded like it was a million miles away.

I moaned, shaking my head.

"Wake up, Race. I'm not done with you yet," she whispered again.

My eyes flew open at a burning so intense that it ripped through my chest. She'd pushed her finger against the cut on my chest.

Everything hit me like a ton of bricks.

My awareness of my surroundings, the smell of her perfume, the sheer pain from the cut, and my absolute terror.

I pulled in a ragged breath before shrieking from the pain.

I mumbled something I didn't even understand as the tears began to flow again.

"See what happens when bitches like you try to steal my husband?"

"No," I screamed, shaking my head.

Just as she started to rip my pants from my body, the door burst open and slammed against the wall.

I turned my head toward the noise, seeing Morgan run through the door. Before he could take a step inside, Natasha held the knife to my throat.

"Take one more step and I'll cut her throat." She pressed the blade against my artery.

I lifted my chin, trying to escape and prevent the crazy bitch from cutting me, and pleaded for Morgan to save me using only my eyes.

Tears streamed down, covering my cheeks as I whimpered. "Please," I whispered to Morgan.

His eyes darted to me, growing wide as he took in the sight of me.

"Put the knife down," a man said as he pushed past Morgan. Tyler O'Shea stopped as soon as he saw me. "What the hell did you do, Natasha?" he asked as his mouth hung open.

"How do you like how your whore looks now, Tyler?" she asked, holding the knife closer to my throat. "Doesn't she look pretty now?"

"Natasha," he whispered.

"Do you want to fuck her now?" She glared at him.

"Morgan," I pleaded, tears falling faster than they had before.

I stared at Morgan, trying to get lost in his eyes as a group of men gathered behind him with the same look of shock and disgust on their faces.

"Put the knife down, baby. We can talk about this. She means nothing to me," Tyler told her, taking a step closer.

"Liar. So, if I did this"—she pushed the blade into my skin and I yelped—"you wouldn't care?"

"Stop," Tyler yelled, holding his hands out.

In one quick move, Morgan pushed Tyler to the side and took aim at Natasha. I held my breath, waiting for the knife to slice my throat.

As the gun went off, I screamed and blacked out.

"Race," a voice whispered in my ear, but this time, it was a man waking me. "Princess, can you hear me?" He stroked my face.

"Mmm," I moaned, unable to speak and too fuckin' scared to open my eyes as the noises around me grew louder.

Someone was undoing my hands and feet as the man continued to touch me with tenderness. "Race, wake up. You're safe," he said in a gentle voice. "Come on, baby."

I know that voice.

Morgan is touching me.

I am safe.

I don't have to be afraid anymore.

"Morgan," I whispered as my eyes fluttered open.

Pain was etched all over his face.

Maybe it was disgust in his eyes at seeing my wounds up close, but he didn't look at me the way he had in my office earlier today.

"Natasha," I whispered as he lifted me off the table.

"She's dead." He clutched me to his chest.

I settled into his warm arms and let my eyes close. Although I was in more pain than I'd ever experienced in my life, I knew no one would hurt me anymore.

"Rest, Race. I have you," he said, walking with me in his arms and kissing my forehead.

"Morgan." I nuzzled as close to his skin as humanly possible.

"I'm here." He rested his head against mine.

"I'm sorry," I said, feeling completely exhausted.

"There's nothing to be sorry about, Race. This is all my fault," he said as he placed me on his lap.

"No." I crawled closer to his side. "Don't put me down."

"I'll never let you go," he murmured, holding me tight.

"You guys go ahead. I'll deal with the police," someone said before the car door slammed.

I jumped.

"I have you." He pulled me into his side, adjusting me in his lap and closing my blouse. "Close your eyes."

I did as he'd said, too tired to argue or try to stay awake.

It was easier when I slept—or, hell, blacked out. I didn't feel the pain from the cuts, panic didn't rattle my body, and I sure as hell didn't have to think.

The only things I needed to know were that Natasha was dead and I was in Morgan's arms.

He'd saved me.

But I wasn't the girl I was before. The look when he saw me would be forever burned in my memory.

CHAPTER TWENTY-EIGHT
MORGAN

Dreams and Nightmares

It had been three weeks since Natasha had abducted Race. I hadn't seen her since I'd carried her into the emergency room and placed her on a gurney. I'd stayed day and night at the hospital, pacing the floors and driving the staff crazy. I'd pleaded with the doctors to let me see her, but she'd left strict orders not to let anyone into her room.

After three days, I finally went home to shower, and by the time I returned, Race was gone.

I called and I texted.

I even left messages at her work, but she hadn't reached out to me.

I sulked for the first week, got pissed by week two, and by the time week three rolled around, I could barely eat.

The only thing that made me get out of bed each morning was my job. The guys were great to me, constantly reassuring me that she'd come back.

I jumped when my phone rang. "Hello?" I said, feeling butterflies in my stomach.

"Yo. Where the fuck are ya, cousin?" Mike asked as he chewed something.

I sighed, feeling a knot form where the butterflies just were. "I'm not in the mood today, Mike."

"Dude, your ma said you better get your ass over here or she's coming to get you." He covered the phone with his hand. "I told him," he said.

"Tell Ma I'll see her another day. I'm just not into family time." I stretched out on the couch, barely able to keep my eyes open.

"Oh shit," he blurted. "Now, my ma said she's coming with her. Expect company, man."

I cleared my throat, throwing my arm over my face to block the sun out. "Tell them to stay there. I'll be there next week."

"He said next week, Auntie Fran." He paused. "Yeah, I'll tell him. Your ma just said she ain't taking no for an answer. You were warned," he said, and then the call disconnected.

I dropped the phone next to my head onto the couch.

I wanted to be alone.

The only person in the world I wanted to see was Race.

I pictured her smiling face, the smell of her skin, and felt the warmth of my fingers gliding across her flesh as I dozed off, losing myself in her.

I closed my eyes, wanting to dream for the first time since I'd been released from active duty. She came to me in sleep. I'd sleep my life away if it meant seeing her.

CHAPTER TWENTY-NINE

RACE

Fran DeLuca

The cuts above my breasts were mostly healed, but they'd never go away.

I ran my fingers along them, feeling the difference in the skin.

I grimaced, hating how they looked.

The skin was pinker and there was a glossy sheen where she'd cut me.

I couldn't let him see me like this.

He'd called twice today and texted me three times.

No matter how many times he tried, I just couldn't answer the phone.

I wanted to hear his voice.

Being in his arms, him whispering in my ear, would make everything melt away.

But I couldn't.

I wasn't ready to see him.

Especially the way I knew we'd end up.

I'd always liked my body, but now, it was just a reminder of that day.

I let myself cry.

I shed tears over Morgan, mostly.

I missed him.

He made me feel safe. I knew he just wanted the best for me.

He hadn't done anything to hurt me.

No.

That was all Natasha.

The wicked bitch would always be with me every time I looked down at my chest.

Natasha haunted my nightmares. I'd relived the night more times than I cared to remember. Each time, I'd wake up in tears with the sheets soaked.

That was when it was the hardest not to call him. I wanted him to hold me, to chase away the demons, and to save me like he had before.

Days turned into nights and hours turned into weeks as I sat on the couch staring at the television.

When I heard a car door close in my driveway, I shot up, trying to catch a glimpse of the person before they knocked.

Butterflies fluttered inside me until I realized it wasn't him.

I'd seen a photo of her before. I opened the door, not waiting for her to knock.

"Hello," I said, my voice a bit shaky.

"Hello, Race. I'm sorry to bother you, dear, but we need to talk."

I glanced around the yard. "Is he here with you?"

She shook her head and frowned. "No. I'm sorry."

Instantly, the excitement I'd felt died. "Would you like to come in, Mrs. DeLuca?" I opened the door for her.

She looked down at her feet and back at me. "I can stay out here if it's easier for you."

"Please come in. I'd rather stay inside if that's okay with you," I said, backing away.

She closed the door, looking around my home. This gave me the opportunity to get a good look at the woman behind the man. She looked the same as her photo, maybe a few years older but just as beautiful.

She wore a pair of washed-out jeans with a black blouse and wedge heels. Her hair was much like his in color, with every hair in place and cut near her shoulders.

"You have a lovely home," she said as she set her purse down on the coffee table.

"Thank you." I sat down. "Did Morgan send you?"

She sat down next to me, patting my leg. "No, dear. He has no idea I'm here."

I sighed as my shoulders sagged. "What can I do for you, Mrs. DeLuca?"

She turned toward me, smoothing her jeans out. "I want to talk to you about my son." She smiled at me. "I hope I'm not being nosy."

"You are." I laughed. "He told me about you."

"He's a little shit."

"He can be that, but he loves you though."

She took a deep breath. "He loves you too, Race."

I swallowed hard, trying to breathe. "He loves me?" I asked.

"Yes. He's been a mess since the day he found you."

"I'm sorry," I whispered and chewed my lip.

"He won't even come to Sunday dinner anymore. He's been grouchy, not sleeping well, barely eating, and just surviving without you."

"Oh," I mumbled. "I feel horrible."

She touched my leg, resting her hand on my knee. "So does he. He's hurting without you, Race."

"I miss him. I just can't let him see me like this." I motioned toward my chest.

"Baby girl," she whispered, tilting her head. "There's nothing to be ashamed of. If a man truly loves you, things like that will never matter."

"I'm scarred," I whispered, not trusting my voice.

"Did you ever think about having a baby?" she asked, staring at me with her lips set in a firm line.

"Someday."

"When you get pregnant and your belly grows big, your entire midsection will stretch. Even after you deliver the baby, the stretch marks will be there forever. Are those scars ugly?"

"Well, no, but those are from something beautiful. They're like a badge of honor earned from giving birth to another little being."

She squeezed my knee. "They're no different than these scars on your skin, my dear. You lived through something and should be proud of yourself for being a survivor."

I shook my head, glancing down at my chest. "It's not the same."

She touched my chin, bringing my eyes to hers. "It is the same. You should be proud that you're a survivor. It's only skin. What matters is what's inside your heart, Race. Do you love him?" she asked, watching me closely.

I swallowed, understanding what she meant. "Yes," I said, giving her a weak smile. "So much it makes my heart hurt."

"You need to go to him."

"I can't." I shook my head. "Not yet."

"If you wait too long, you may lose him forever."

Tears stung my eyes and slid down my cheeks.

"Don't cry." She wrapped her arm around my shoulder and pulled my face to her chest. "He blames himself for what happened to you."

I sucked in a breath, feeling like someone had kicked me in the gut. "Why?"

The tears fell faster, dropping onto her jeans.

"He didn't get there in time to save you."

"But he did. She would've killed me," I said, clutching my throat.

"He thinks he failed you. He assumes that's why you won't talk to him." She rubbed my back. "Sometimes our head gets in the way of our heart. He's reached out to you. Now, it's time for you to talk to him. Let him know that you don't blame him."

I cried harder. I'd put him through more heartache. I needed him as much as he needed me.

I wiped the tears away, sitting up. "You're right, Mrs. DeLuca. I need to see him. He needs to know I love him and I don't blame him for anything."

"Let's get you ready. I'll take you there. We'll surprise him."

"Um, he doesn't seem like the type to enjoy surprises," I mumbled, wiping my face.

"There's no time like the present. Imagine how happy you'll make him if you show up at his door. Up you go." She pushed me off the couch.

I stood, glancing down at her. "Are you sure about this? Because—"

She nodded, climbing to her feet. "If there's one thing I know, it's my son. He's in love with you, sweet girl," she said, holding my shoulders. "I want to make him happy."

"I want him happy too," I said as she turned me around, using my shoulders to push me toward the hallway.

"Then go get ready. We have a boy to see."

CHAPTER THIRTY

MORGAN

Paradise Found

"**O**pen the goddamn door!" Ma pounded on my door and woke me from my dream.

"Fuck." I stared at the ceiling, running my hands down my face.

She'd shown up about the same time shit had gone south with Race. I'd spent the last twenty-one days trying to avoid her as much as possible. She made it harder and harder, showing up at my house unexpectedly or "popping in" to the office to say hello.

I never thought I'd say this, but I longed for my army days when shit was simpler.

When my heart wasn't in the hands of a woman and my ma was thousands of miles away.

Everything was complicated now.

Everything.

I yearned for the simpler days.

"I'm coming." I climbed to my feet and cracked my neck.

"You better open this damn door," she yelled again, continuing her pounding.

"Coming, Ma." I thought about escaping out the back door before I flung the door open just as her hand was about to land another blow, but instead, it hit me in the chest.

"Sorry, baby," she muttered as she glanced up at me. "Jesus, you look like shit."

"Thanks, Ma. You always know the right words to say."

"Look at you." She motioned toward my face and the stubble I'd let grow since Friday. "We gotta get you cleaned up," she said as she took my hand and led me into my living room.

"Hey." Auntie Mar took a step into my house.

"Hi, Auntie Mar," I said in a less-than-enthused voice.

"We have someone here to see you. You need to look better than this." Ma dragged me toward my bedroom.

"Who?" I asked, feeling my stomach turn over and looking over my shoulder.

"A friend."

"Ma…" I wasn't in the mood for her games.

She pulled me into the bedroom and closed the door. "You seemed so sad, love. I had to do something."

I shook my head, hoping she'd stuck her nose in where I'd never wanted her to stick it before. "What did you do, Ma?"

"I had a little talk with your girl."

"What?" I was both excited and shocked. "Is she here?" I took a step toward the door, but Ma blocked it.

"She is, but she can't see you like this."

"Jesus. I look like hell," I said as I caught a glimpse of myself in the full-length mirror.

I ripped my shirt off and ran into my bathroom. "Why didn't you tell me she was here?" I mumbled as I brushed my teeth.

"It would've ruined the fun." Her laughter carried into the bathroom.

"Now isn't the time for jokes. She better be out there. So help me God, if you're joking..." Then I took a sip of water and spat it in the sink.

"She's here. Aren't you glad I'm a nosy mom now?"

I closed my eyes, hardly able to believe what I was about to say. "For once, I couldn't be happier that you're so far up my ass I can barely breathe." I ran my fingers through my hair, smelled my armpits, and winced.

God, I sure as hell wasn't fresh.

I threw some deodorant on and grabbed a shirt from the back of the bathroom door.

"Let me out there," I told her as she still stood in front of the door.

She nodded. "We're going to leave you two here alone. When you're done, come back to the house for supper."

"It's almost four, Ma. It's past Gallo time." I lifted her from in front of the door and set her to the side.

"Your aunt postponed dinner until six tonight just for you and Race."

"What?"

"We've had this up our sleeve all weekend, baby. Now, you go make up with Race and come back to us."

I grabbed the door handle and glanced over my shoulder at her. "I love her, Ma."

"I know you do. Go get her, son."

"On it," I called out as I walked into the living room.

Before I turned the corner, I could see her reflection in the hallway mirror.

Standing with her hands clutched in front of her, she didn't look like the tough chick I'd fallen for over a month ago.

I took two steps forward, clearing my throat, and waited for her eyes to meet mine.

God, she was beautiful.

The sun streamed through the windows, lighting her outline and making it look as if she were glowing.

Her head rose slowly, and she met my gaze. Across the room, I could see the tears start to form and spill down her cheeks.

"Let's leave these two kids alone." Auntie Mar pulled my ma toward the doorway. "They can handle things on their own."

"Race," I called out, stepping toward her.

"Morgan." Her bottom lip trembled.

She leaped into my arms.

I wrapped my arms around her, holding her body against mine and burying my face in her hair. She smelled just as I remembered.

"I've been worried about you, princess." I inhaled her sweetness.

"I'm sorry." She wrapped her legs around my back and rested her forehead against my chin. "I'm so sorry."

"I'm so happy that you're here. Nothing else matters."

"I'm sorry," she repeated. Then she started to sob, shaking in my arms.

"Baby," I whispered. "Shh. Don't cry." I carried her to the couch, placed her in my lap, and cradled her.

"I shouldn't have ignored you." Her arms wrapped around my neck and she nuzzled into my skin. "I've been a horrible person."

"Come on now. Stop that. You're here now. I have you. You're mine, Race." I leaned back, taking her with me.

"I know. I've been so selfish." She sobbed, tears landing on my shirt as she cried.

"Race," I whispered, rocking back and forth, trying to comfort us both. I let her cry and held her tight. I didn't care about the tears or the fact that she'd used my T-shirt as a Kleenex. I was just happy to have her in my arms.

When she stopped, she pushed herself up, using my chest as leverage. "Can you forgive me?"

I stroked her cheek with the back of my knuckles. "For what?"

"For ignoring you. You saved me and—"

I pressed my finger against her lips. "Don't say it. It's in the past. What's done is done."

"I'm sorry," she mumbled against my index finger.

There's my girl.

Race was here. She was safe, and she was in my arms. "Are you okay?"

She nodded, giving me a small flicker of a smile. "I don't want you to see my body again."

I frowned as I stared into her eyes. "Is that what you're worried about?"

She nodded again, looking at me from under her eyelashes. "I look like a monster."

I touched her chin, bringing her eyes back to mine. "Don't ever say such a thing. You're a beautiful person. We all have scars. Some we can see and others we can't. Wear those with pride. You went through something so horrible and survived it, Race."

Tears started to form again and threatened to fall. "I've been in therapy," she said, swallowing back the tears.

"Good."

"She's helped me."

"I'm proud of you." I leaned forward and kissed her forehead. "I've missed you," I said against her skin. "Are you healed?"

"Almost. I talked with a plastic surgeon, and I'll always have them."

"Scars don't scare me." I wanted to take her pain away, remove the scars from her body, and put them on my own. I could live with them, but Race had been through so much already. "Can I see them?"

She sat up and stared at me. "Not yet, Morgan. I'm not ready for anyone to see them."

I nodded. "When you're ready. Promise me you won't disappear again. If you do, I won't let you hide."

"I won't."

"Come here." I pulled her toward me and laid her head on my chest. "I want to hold you for a little while." I reclined our bodies, placing her on top of me as I spread out on the couch.

She relaxed into me, toying with my shirt. I closed my eyes, feeling her warmth.

I didn't care if she kissed me or if we had sex. I just wanted to hold her.

When I woke, I watched her sleep. Tiny snores fell from her lips as she inhaled through her nose, followed by a tiny puff of air coming out of her mouth.

Her top had shifted while we'd slept, exposing the edge of the scars near the center of her chest.

They were faint, much lighter than I had expected.

I pushed her top back and traced the lines, feeling their smoothness under my fingertips.

Leaning forward, I touched my lips to the one above her left breast and kissed it. She stirred, and I stilled, trying to avoid waking her.

"Morgan," she whispered.

I glanced up, my lips still against her freshly healed wound. "Sorry I woke you," I murmured against her skin.

"What are you doing?" She yawned.

"I wanted to kiss you."

She shifted, trying to move away from me.

I held her tighter, looking up at her. "I wanted to see, Race. I couldn't stop from touching them."

She stiffened. "Why?"

"They're part of you. I never want to forget that I almost lost you."

"But they're ugly," she said as her lip trembled.

"No, they're not. I love every inch of your body," I said, and I laid my lips upon the very spot she hated most.

"I don't know how you can look at me."

"There isn't a spot on your body I wouldn't kiss. Everything about you is beautiful."

"You just want to get in my pants again," she whispered as she started to giggle.

"Well. That too."

"So you don't think I'm ugly?"

I nudged her shirt open with my nose, exposing more of the scars. "I love you, Race True. Every. Single. Inch," I murmured against her skin as I placed tiny kisses along the lines.

Tears started to stream down her cheeks. "I love you too, Morgan DeLuca. Will you do something for me?" She wiped away the tears from her face.

"Anything." I glanced up at her.

"Make love to me," she whispered, running her fingers through my hair.

Without waiting another moment, I moved up her body and settled my mouth over hers.

I kissed her like my life depended on it, sharing the very air we breathed.

I didn't fuck Race True.

No.

I made love to my woman.

CHAPTER
THIRTY-ONE

MORGAN

Sweet as Sugar

Race fidgeted with her hands. "Shit, I'm so nervous."

"Why?" I stopped walking and turned to face her. "You've met Ma and Auntie Mar, and without me, too. They're the toughest."

She shook her head. "It was different."

"You weren't mine?" A smile crept across my face and I cupped her cheek.

"Yes. I mean, this is your family," she said, glancing toward the sky. "What if they hate me?"

I brushed her lips with mine. "They won't hate you."

"Liar," she teased. "We didn't make it to dinner last week."

I couldn't hide my amusement as I chuckled. "I explained things. They understood, princess. They thought we were busy."

"Oh my God. They thought we were having sex?" Her mouth hung open.

"No." They probably did think that. "They know we fell asleep."

"Uh-huh," she muttered and then sighed.

I grabbed her hand, holding it tight. "Come on before they come outside to get us. They're probably all watching from the windows."

"You know I love your ma." She walked beside me, squeezing my hand.

"You do?" I glanced at her.

"Yeah. She calls me every day to check on me."

"Fuckin' great," I mumbled as we approached the door.

"You don't know how lucky you are to have such a loving mom."

"Is that what she is now?"

Fran found a way to weave herself into every part of my life. The only sanctuaries I now had were at work and home, and even then, she'd barge in to check on me.

"Stop being a jerk. Fran loves you." Race wrapped her arms around my waist, resting her head on my chest.

I tangled my fingers in her hair and hugged her. "I'm a little worried you're on a first-name basis with my ma," I said.

"Morgan," she whispered, peering up at me. "I don't talk to my mom, so it's nice to have yours to talk to every day."

"She has plenty of love to give, princess." Maybe if Ma focused some on Race, she'd get off my back for a little while.

The front door opened and, like clockwork, Ma appeared. "There you two are," she said, holding her arms out.

Race released me, drifting to Ma as I watched. Ma had met very few women in my life, but this was the first time she'd welcomed one.

"It's good to see you, sweetie," Ma said, patting Race on the back and sticking her tongue out at me. "We've been waiting for the both of you."

"Sorry we're late, Fran. It won't happen again," Race said as she backed away.

"Oh, honey, you're fine." Ma smiled at me, repeating the gesture and holding her arms out.

"Ma, I've missed you," I said sarcastically as I let her hug me.

"Don't be late again," she whispered in my ear. "Aunt Mar will have a cow."

"But I thought—"

"You know better than to be late."

To Race, she was as sweet as sugar, but to me, her stinger came out and the old Fran appeared.

It didn't matter.

I appreciated the fact that Ma liked Race and treated her differently, even if I received the same old treatment.

"Okay, Ma," I said, not willing to argue and ready to see the rest of the family.

I'd seen James and Thomas every day at the office, but I'd missed my other cousins and my aunt and uncle.

In Chicago, I'd barely thought about them, with scattered phone calls and greeting cards throughout the year. Now that they were back in my life, there was nothing I wanted to do more on a Sunday than have family time.

After my dad had left—don't get me started on the rat bastard—family meals were never the same. Ma and I had sat around and stared at each other before I'd headed off to basic training. Life had changed in a hurry.

I realized I needed to cut Fran some slack.

Not only had her husband left her, but in a very short time after that, I had too. Her world had crumbled. Everything she loved had disappeared, and she had been left alone.

"I love you, Ma," I blurted out, giving her a final squeeze.

"Where did that come from?" She backed away from me and gawked.

"Nowhere. Just thought I should tell you more."

"You should," she replied in true Fran fashion. "I spent hours giving birth to you. Painful hours." She guided us into the house. "They're here!" she yelled in the foyer, the sound echoing through the space.

Ma stood on her tiptoes, putting her mouth next to my ear. "I told them not to scare Race," she whispered.

I gave her a brief nod.

Ma wasn't always a pain in the ass. More often than not she was, but there was also a thoughtful side to Fran DeLuca.

Times like these reminded me why I was thankful she was mine.

I put my arm around Race's shoulder as she glanced up at me. "You're going to be fine," I told her as we walked into the living room.

"Morgan." Izzy handed one of the babies off before walking over to us. "Race, it's good to meet you." She smiled at Race and hugged her. "Good to see you too, cousin."

James held both boys in his arms, looking content. "Yo!" he said, sounding a little like Mike.

I nodded then turned my attention toward Uncle Sal.

"Son," Uncle Sal called out as he approached me, holding his hand out.

I placed my hand in his and shook. "Hey, Uncle Sal."

He pulled me against him and gave me a hug. "I'm glad you're here, Morgan. We missed you the last month."

"I know. I'm so sorry for everything that's happened."

He shook his head and stared at me, rubbing his chin. "Don't be sorry. You're here now."

"Morgan," Auntie Mar chimed from the kitchen doorway. "I made your favorite." She winked.

"You're the best, Auntie Mar." I blew her a kiss.

An elbow smashed into my ribs. "Hey now," Ma warned, poking me again with that bony thing.

"I'm kidding, Ma," I lied. Then gave her a kiss on the cheek.

"How are you, dear?" Auntie Mar hugged Race.

"I'm well, Mrs. Gallo. I head back to work tomorrow, which is a little scary."

"You'll be fine, dear. Keep your head held high," Auntie Mar said as she rubbed Race's back.

Race waved as everyone stared at her. "Hey, everyone. I'm Race," she said as she elbowed me in the ribs. "Morgan seems to have forgotten his manners."

I grimaced. "Sorry, princess."

I'd just been so happy that I'd totally forgotten she hadn't met everyone.

To my utter disbelief, I felt more content than I had in...well...forever.

"I envy you," Race told Mia as we sat on the lanai after dinner.

I could barely move.

My stomach hadn't consumed that much food for as long as I could remember. It was hard to resist my aunt's cooking, especially when she'd gone above and beyond this week because of Race.

"Me?" Mia placed her hand on her chest.

Race nodded as she took a sip of her wine. "You have your own business. You don't need to deal with anyone's BS."

"Mama, mama," Lily, Mia's daughter, whined next to her, holding her arms out and shaking them.

Mia smiled at Lily before looking back to Race. "Why don't you just quit?" Mia suggested as she pulled Lily into her lap.

Race scrubbed her face with her hands and sighed. "I've worked my butt off to get where I am. I can't imagine just walking away."

"Do you love it?" Mia asked.

"My work?"

"Yeah. Do you love it?"

"Ugh," Race muttered. "I used to, but I don't know anymore."

"I'm sure what you've been through changes things."

"So, dude, when are we going to go out?" Mike elbowed me.

"What?" I asked, too busy listening to the ladies talk to have heard Mike's question.

"I want to hang out."

"Oh." I glanced over at him. "I'm so busy between work and Race. Sorry I haven't been around."

Mike nodded. "I get it." He motioned toward Race. "New love."

"As soon as stuff levels out, we'll have a guys' night out."

"Maybe we can get everyone to go." He smiled,

looking around at his brothers. "Kids have put a damper on everything."

I peered over at Mia after he spoke. "How would you know?" she asked, glaring at him. "It's not like you've even changed a diaper in your life."

Mike blanched. "Have you smelled what comes out of those little things? I don't have the stomach for it," Mike said, waving his hands.

"For such a big guy, you sure are a sissy," I teased Mike.

"You change her, then." He pointed at the beautiful little Lily, with her wild, curly, dark hair as she sat in her mother's lap.

"Daddy sissy," Lily said.

"Lily," Mike said.

"Daddy sissy." Lily giggled, staring up at Mia.

"Great, man. Nice job," Mike muttered as his shoulders sagged.

"Baby, Daddy isn't a sissy. Look at how big and tough he is," Mia said as she glanced over at Mike.

Growling, Mike flexed. "That's right, baby. Daddy is tough." Mike stared down at his biceps, watching them jump.

"Daddy sissy," Lily repeated as her giggles grew louder.

"Jesus." Mike scrubbed a hand down his face.

Race giggled, covering her mouth as tears started to form in her eyes. She mouthed "Thank you" to me.

We stayed on the lanai, chatting until the sun hung low in the sky and dusk started to settle across the backyard.

"We better get going, princess. You have to be up early for work." I pushed my chair back.

"But I don't want to go," she whined as she climbed from her seat.

"Be a good girl and I'll give you a reward," I said, giving her a wink. "If you're a really good girl, I'll give you a spanking."

"Mama, why would Morgan spank Race if she's good?" Tamara asked Max, her face scrunched up and her tiny nose wrinkled.

Anthony patted Tamara's head, glaring at me. "Thanks for that, Morgan."

Max knelt down, bringing herself eye level with Tamara. "Sweetheart, Morgan was just kidding."

"But when I'm bad, Daddy says he's going to spank me." Tamara looked at me from the corner of her eye. "He doesn't look like he's kidding, Mama. Morgan is kind of scary," she whispered to Max, but it was loud enough that everyone could hear.

I found the entire thing priceless.

"Don't worry, Tamara," Race said as she looked down at her. "Morgan is like a teddy bear. Don't listen to him. He just acts tough."

"Like Uncle Joey?" Tamara asked, glancing over at Joe.

"Just like him, dollface." Race tapped Tamara on the nose. "Should I give him a spanking for scaring you?" Race looked up at me, her green eyes twinkling.

Tamara pulled at her lip, nodding slowly. "You should," she replied as a lopsided smile formed on her face. "If he's been a bad boy, then he deserves it."

"Oh, baby, he's been a very bad boy." Race winked at me as she stood. "I'll take care of him."

Tamara turned her body from side to side as she giggled. "Morgan's going to get punished," she said cheerfully.

"Only if I'm lucky." I patted Tamara on the head as I kissed Max. "Sorry, babe," I whispered in her ear.

"Oh, please. Anthony says things that are ten times worse." Max kissed my cheek. "I'm sure she's going to be very confused when she gets older."

"Yeah. Or she'll realize how sick we all are."

"Ready to go home, Mara?" Anthony picked the little girl up and placed her on his hip.

She tugged at his ear, resting her head on his shoulder. "Yeah, Daddy. Will you sing for me tonight?"

"Which one, baby?" He kissed the top of her head.

"The one you and Mommy danced to at your wedding." Tamara grabbed his face between her tiny hands. "Please, Daddy."

"Anything you want, baby girl."

"Sounds like you have a busy night in front of you, cousin," I said as I walked up to him. "I'll see you next week."

He held his hand out. "I wouldn't trade nights like this for anything in the world."

"I'll take your word for it." I shook his hand.

"There's nothing like the first time your daughter says, 'I love you.' You realize there's no other love like it." He clutched Tamara a little closer.

I dropped my hands, realizing that my cousin had everything in the world. A loving wife, a child, and an amazing family.

"You're a lucky man, Anthony."

"I imagine you're not too far off from where I'm standing."

I shook my head. "I'm at the starting line."

"It's not a marathon."

"I'm not sprinting."

"Just don't wait until you're as old as I am to realize

you've wasted years running from the thing that makes you the happiest."

I glanced over at Race, taking his words in and knowing he was right.

No matter what, I was nothing alone.

The one thing in the world that made me feel complete stood across the table, laughing with my family.

I wouldn't let her get away.

Being apart for three weeks made me realize that I didn't want to be alone anymore.

CHAPTER THIRTY-TWO

RACE

Hard Choices

A warmth between my legs woke me from my slumber. My eyes fluttered open and a moan escaped my lips as his tongue circled my clit.

I closed my eyes, pushing my body down against his face.

This was better than any cup of coffee I'd ever had, the way I wished I could wake up every morning.

He gripped my thighs, holding my legs open as he licked me. Clutching the sheets in my hands, I arched my back and struggled to catch my breath.

As my toes started to curl, his mouth left me.

"Don't stop," I pleaded, lifting my head from the pillow.

"I have to be inside you," he murmured as he crawled up my body.

Before I started to whine, he rubbed the head of his cock through my wetness and plunged inside.

"Yes!" I cried out, the feel of his mouth on me quickly forgotten.

He placed his arm behind my back, drawing me closer to him. When his hand slid under my ass, tilting my hips, his dick went deeper.

"Oh," I breathed, loving the feel of him inside me. I wrapped my legs around his back, drawing him to me as he thrust inside me over and over again.

Our skin grew damp, both of our bodies shaking as we came together. For the first time in my life, I actually had an orgasm at the same time as the man I was with. It was like the clouds parted, the heavens shone, and the angels sang.

"Damn," he murmured against my lips, his breath skidding across my face.

"Mm," I replied, unable to say anything else.

"Now that's the way to start a week," he whispered, rolling to his side.

"Ugh. Don't remind me."

"Still don't want to go to work?" He pulled me to his side with the arm that was lodged under my back.

"No, but I have to." I nestled my cheek against his chest.

"Want me to drop by and see you today?" He brushed his lips against my forehead.

"No. I'll be okay." I didn't know if I could handle going back.

Everyone in the office knew what had happened with Natasha. There was no way to hide it, and I knew that it would be on everyone's mind today as they looked at me. I wondered if they'd ever forget.

It had made all the papers. I hadn't even left my house for a week after I'd been released from the hospital. I hadn't wanted people to stare at me. I'd figured that after ten days, people had moved on to the next big story and had forgotten all about me.

When I did venture out, I still felt like everyone was staring at me. I knew they weren't, but I couldn't convince myself otherwise.

If it weren't for Morgan, I might have become a shut-in.

Let me rephrase that. If it weren't for Morgan's mother, I might have been perfectly content to stay in my home forever. She came to me, held me while I cried, and helped me pick up the pieces.

Without her, I wouldn't have been lying in his arms and feeling the peace that had just washed over me.

"I'm just a phone call away, princess. If you need me, I'll rush to your side." His other hand touched my arm, gently rubbing it as my body was flush to his.

"It'll be okay." I didn't know if I was trying to convince him or me. "I'm tougher than this. Damn," I mumbled.

"You're one of the toughest women I know. Remember that. You can do anything you want."

"Even quit?" I asked, glancing up at him.

"Quit if you want, princess. Don't do something you don't want to anymore."

I chewed my lip, wondering if I'd have the guts to quit and never look back without regret. "Easy for you to say," I said, rolling my eyes.

"See how today goes. You may have an easier time saying those words than you think. If you can't handle it today, then don't go back. Life's too damn short to be unhappy."

"I have a meeting with my boss at eleven. I'll see how I feel then."

Months ago, I would've said that nothing in the world could make me quit, but that had changed. Looking into the face of death had made me reevaluate my life. No longer did I find joy in my work—instead, I found peace in life's simple moments.

"You call and I'll be there, babe."

"I know you will," I whispered, wrapping my arm around him and squeezing him. "I love you, Morgan."

"Princess," he whispered, dragging my face to his. As he stared down at me, he smiled. "I love you too, Race. More than I've ever loved anyone or anything in the entire world."

I reached up and gave him a kiss.

Best Monday ever.

Worst Monday ever.

When the elevator doors opened this morning, it sounded like everything in the office stopped. It was like being in a movie. As I walked by, every person turned to face me, papers fluttered to the floor, and people whispered to each other.

I knew that it wasn't really happening, but it felt that way to me. I felt every eye on me as I walked toward my office door. People nodded, giving me a sad smile as if they felt sorry for me. I held my head up high, refusing to play the role of the victim as I marched toward my office.

"Hi, Cara." I stopped at her desk. "Please give me a few moments to myself."

"So glad to see you, Ms. True," she replied as she nodded. "You take all the time you need, honey."

I turned on my heel and walked into my office, closing the door quietly behind me. My back collapsed against the door as I used it to hold myself up.

I couldn't do this.

I didn't want to do this.

I hated it here.

The last time I had been in this room, Natasha was with me. Even though she was dead, her words and actions haunted me.

I didn't want to be *that* girl.

I wasn't her.

I was Race—the tough chick that people cowered in front of, the one who bossed people around and exuded confidence. Not the girl who needed a door to hold myself up as I found the strength to take another step.

I glanced at the clock on the wall behind my desk, realizing I had two hours before the meeting with Mr. Emerson. Maybe I'd feel different if I immersed myself in my work, letting my mind focus only on the task at hand.

It'll only be tough for the first day.

If I could only get through this day, tomorrow would be easier. Just one day. Just like my therapist had told me.

Even over the last four weeks, small tasks had become simpler and I'd found myself feeling like I had before the attack. But that was at home, running to the store, or spending time with Morgan.

Coming back to work was like starting again at square one. I had to take baby steps to become the kickass businesswoman I had always been.

I was Race True.

Strong.

Smart.

Feared.

"Race." Cara's muffled voice came from the other side of the door as she knocked.

I pushed off the door and strode toward my desk as I tossed my purse on the couch. "Come in," I replied, running my fingers against the cool glass of the desktop.

Cara entered. After taking two steps, she stopped. "What's wrong?" She frowned.

"Nothing, Cara," I replied, glancing out the window.

"Come on now. I can always tell when there's something you aren't saying." She walked toward her usual chair.

"I just don't feel at home here anymore." I sat down, testing my chair as I rocked back and forth.

"You were meant for bigger things," Cara said as she looked around. "You weren't meant to be cooped up in a place like this. You should be running your own company."

"Now you're just being silly, Cara." I leaned back in my chair, thinking about what she'd said. "What's my schedule today?"

She stared down at her legal pad, tapping her pencil against the surface. "It's pretty light. I didn't want to overburden you today." She glanced up at me.

I returned her smile, though mine was less believable. "Thanks. What's first?"

"You have a meeting with Sue in development at ten and Mr. Emerson at eleven. Your afternoon is free because I didn't know if you'd make it a full day," she said, peering down at the paper.

"I think I'm just nervous about meeting with Emerson. I'll feel better when that's over, I'm sure."

"I'm sure," she repeated, standing from the chair. "Would you like me to get you a cup of coffee?" she asked as she strolled toward the door.

"That would be lovely, Cara."

"Coming right up, Ms. True."

With that, she disappeared.

Maybe a little kick of caffeine would have me feeling like my old self again. Or after I listened to Sue drone on for an hour, I'd be so bored and annoyed I'd want to throat-punch someone.

It had been a long time since I'd felt that fire burn deep in my belly. The old me had it smoldering, ready to explode at any moment.

I turned my computer on, ready to bury myself in my work and find the slow burn again. I wouldn't let them defeat me.

"Mr. Emerson will see you now," his secretary said, raking her eyes over my body with her lips set in a firm line.

As I walked through the doors of his office, I knew exactly what I needed to do.

CHAPTER THIRTY-THREE

MORGAN

A Little Race For Lunch

"Who is he again?" I asked Thomas, glancing down at my clock.

Race and I were meeting for a late lunch today. It was her first day back at work. She promised that she'd be here at two and I shouldn't keep her waiting.

"He's one of Joey's friends from the Neon Cowboy. His name is Frisco."

"Joe vouches for him," James said, raising an eyebrow as he rested his hands behind his head.

Thomas nodded, rubbing the back of his neck.

"Well, you two are the bosses, and if Joe vouches for him, then I'm sure he's a good guy." I knew that Joe didn't like many people.

The door opened and Angel was standing there with a man behind her. "Thomas, Frisco is here." She glanced over her shoulder and stepped aside.

"Frisco." Thomas walked around his desk to greet the newcomer.

"Thomas," he replied, shaking his hand.

I gave him a quick appraisal.

He had a muscular build but a lean frame. He stood pin straight, reminding me of a military man. His eyes never left one of ours, showing he was honest.

"It's great to have you here." Thomas looked over at James. "That's James, and over there," he looked toward me, "is my cousin, Morgan. Guys, this is Frisco."

"Frank is my real name, but I go by Frisco," he said, giving us each a quick nod.

"Come on in, Frisco. We have a lot to discuss," James said.

"Thank you," Thomas said to Angel.

She waved and closed the door, leaving the four of us to speak.

"What's with the name Frisco?" James asked as Frisco sat down. "Was your mom a *General Hospital* fan?"

"I'm from San Fran. The guys at the bar like to use nicknames." He shrugged.

"*GH* is a better angle."

"Let's go over a few rules." Thomas sat down.

"Shoot," Frisco replied, relaxing into his chair.

"First things first. Angel, whom you've met already, is mine. Race, whom you will meet, is Morgan's. Hands off our ladies. Let's just get that free and clear."

He raked his fingers through his hair. "I'm having enough trouble with my woman to even bother thinking about someone else's."

"Why don't you tell us about your skills?" James said, changing the subject.

"I was a Navy man for years, serving as a SEAL. I can't go into detail. Many of my missions are still classified."

I glanced over at Thomas just as he looked at me.

We both had the same impressed look on our faces.

Even though I was an army man through and through, I still had respect for all branches of the service.

SEALs weren't pussies.

"I think I have many of the skills, if not all, that would make me a great PI."

"Full of yourself," I muttered in a low voice.

He glanced at me. "I am," he replied with a smirk. "But I can back that shit up."

"So can I."

"Gentlemen, let's save the attitudes for the bad guys," Thomas said.

"We're cool, man," I said, giving Frisco a nod. "I know that, if he was a SEAL, he can back his shit up, but even if I was only an army grunt, I can too."

"We all have skills," James said. "If any of you didn't, you wouldn't be here."

"Go on." Thomas stared at Frisco and ignored me.

"Whatever you need done, I can do it." Frisco glanced at me out of the corner of his eye. "I'm here to be a team player. I just want to dive in and get my hands dirty."

"Let's just hope your first case doesn't go down like Morgan's," James said, patting me on the back.

"I wouldn't wish that on my worst enemy."

"That bad?" Frisco asked as he grimaced.

"Someday, I'll tell you about her."

"Did you lose her?" he asked, tilting his head. "I couldn't imagine someone dying because I fucked up."

"Nah, man. I didn't lose her. My world has never been the same since the day I was assigned to her case."

"I'm sorry to hear that." Frisco winced.

I remembered how simple shit used to be. "I'm not."

He returned his attention to Thomas. "I'm a pretty straightforward guy. I shoot straight, tell the truth, and sometimes I speak before thinking."

"Sounds like you'll fit right in."

I glanced at my watch again, realizing I was about to be late to my lunch appointment with Race. "I'm gonna run, guys." I stood.

"Try not to take an extended lunch again today," Thomas warned.

"At least I take mine outside of the office," I shot back. "Word to the wise, Frisco. Always knock," I said, holding my hand out.

He gave me a confused look as Thomas and James both laughed. "What?" he asked.

I shook my head. "Never mind. You'll figure it out."

"I have to run too," Thomas said as he walked around his desk. "I have a meeting with a potential client."

"I'll show Frisco the ropes and get him situated," James said.

I snapped my fingers, turning toward Thomas. "I have a meeting tonight with a client. So I plan to take a very long lunch. I'll be back in the office around six."

"Do you need one of us here?" Thomas asked.

"Nah, I got it."

"I'll be around," James added. "Izzy's home with the kids today."

"You better not stay late. She'll murder you if you leave her all day with the boys."

"Let me worry about your sister, Thomas."

"Frisco, if James doesn't come back to work tomorrow because my sister kills him, you can have his office."

"What the fuck?" I pretended to be insulted. "I should get that office first."

"Boys," James interrupted as he headed for the door and opened it. "No one gets my office. Someday you'll learn to handle your women like I do."

Thomas and I burst into laughter.

"He's so full of shit," Thomas said.

I used that as my cue to exit. "I'm out. Catch ya guys later. Nice to meet you, Frisco."

"Bye," he said as I walked out.

As I walked toward my office, Race approached from the waiting room.

"Hey, baby." She wrapped her arms around me.

"Hey, princess. How did work go?" I kissed the top of her head.

She peered up at me. "Fantastic."

"Really?"

She nodded and kept smiling. "Not at first, but it got better."

"Let's go into my office and talk before we head to lunch. Okay?" I asked, opening the door.

"Sure," she said as she stepped inside.

"So, work wasn't as bad as you thought it would be?"

"It was worse." She laughed. "So much worse."

"Okay," I whispered and stroked my chin. "You're acting weird. Why are you so happy if it was worse?"

She sobered as she placed her hands flat on the desk and leaned over. "Because I quit!" she shouted.

"You quit?" Relief washed over me.

"Yes." She stood up, held her arms out, and began to twirl. "I marched into Mr. Emerson's office and told him I was done." She fist-pumped the air.

I'd never seen Race this free and excited about anything before, and I couldn't help but smile. "Wow. That's amazing, babe. I'm so excited for you."

I hadn't been able to get her out of my thoughts this morning. Walking into that office had to be one of the toughest things she'd ever done. Everyone knew about her case; it had been all over the news the next day. She couldn't hide from it, and if her office was as cutthroat as she claimed, I'd expected problems ahead.

She stopped spinning, dropping her arms to her sides and swaying. "I feel free for the first time ever."

I walked over to her, needing to get a little piece of happiness myself. "I'm so proud of you," I told her as I pulled her into my arms.

"We need to celebrate." She giggled as she stared up at me.

"What do you have in mind?" I leaned forward and peppered her neck with kisses.

"Oh, no you don't," she said, trying to get out of my grasp.

I chuckled against her skin. "I can't think of a better way to celebrate."

"You're taking me to lunch." She crawled out of my arms, darting behind me.

"I'd rather have a little Race for lunch," I teased.

"We can't," she said as I tried to grab her, but she moved sideways and out of reach.

"Yes, we can. I've walked in on Thomas and Angel more times than I'd like to remember." I tried to catch her again.

She stopped moving as her mouth dropped open. "You have?"

This time, I didn't miss, grabbing hold of her arms. "Gotcha," I growled. "I have. I fear my office is the only one that hasn't been christened."

She placed her hands on my chest, smiling at me. "I'm afraid that'll have to wait."

"What am I supposed to do with this?" I asked as I rubbed my crotch against her stomach, letting her feel my hard dick.

"Oh," she murmured. "We can't have you going to lunch like that."

I stared into her eyes and pouted. "It would be a shame for it to go to waste. I can't really walk out of here like this, either, princess."

"I suppose you can't," she whispered, rubbing her fingers along my stubble. "Just a quickie. I'm starving."

"Quickie works, but later I expect it long and slow." I groaned as I brushed my mouth against the skin of her face, feeling the silkiness on my lips.

"Have something in mind?" she asked as she tipped her head back, giving me access to her neck.

"I always have a plan," I murmured as I kissed my way to her collarbone, stopping before I got to her scars. "Quickie now to make you happy, and a little something extra later to make me happy," I said before I bit down on her flesh.

She thought about it, her eyes darting around the room. She nodded as she looked into my eyes. "It's a deal."

"Sometimes a deal with the devil isn't always smart." I smirked.

"I think I can take whatever you're giving."

"Don't write checks with your mouth that your ass can't cash."

"What?" she asked, scrunching her nose.

"You'll see."

She threw her head back. "I trust you," she said through her giggles.

I held her ass in my hands and squeezed. "I want to own all of you. I plan to claim every last inch of you tonight."

She gasped. "Oh," she said, her cheeks growing flushed. "You know all the pretty things to say to a lady."

She placed her hand on my chest, her palm scorching my skin through the material.

I placed my mouth over hers and gave her a kiss that stole the air from my lungs.

Fuck, I loved her.

I lifted her in the air as she wrapped her legs around my back, locking our bodies together. Carrying her over to the desk, I placed my mouth on hers, quieting her moans.

Opening one eye, I found the desk and laid her out on top of it.

"Are you sure this is okay?" she asked in a breathy tone.

"Totally sure." I slid my hands up her thighs, finding her garter. "Lie back." I reached the edge of her panties.

"Oh God." She grabbed the edge of the desk.

"Perfect," I murmured as I started to undo my pants and push them down to my ankles. My cock sprang free, harder than ever and ready for action.

Without having to be told, she lifted her ass and shimmied her skirt up to her waist, giving me an amazing view.

"Those have to go." I touched the edge of her black lace panties. As I grabbed the sides, she lifted, allowing me to pull them off. I twirled them in my fingers before throwing them across the room.

"Hey." She turned her head, trying to see where they landed.

"I have a new rule." I leaned over the desk, bringing my lips to hers.

"What's that?" she asked, her breath skating across my face.

"No more panties. They're forbidden."

"You can't just make that rule."

"I did. No more," I growled, moving her mouth with mine.

My palms caressed her breasts, and I rubbed her nipple with my fingertips as I kissed her. As my hand slid down her body, her back arched, moving my hand down.

She was slick and ready when I cupped her pussy.

"This is mine," I said, not really putting it up for debate.

"It's yours," she breathed, arching her back and pushing down against my hand.

"Good girl," I said as I slipped a finger inside.

Her back arched further, pushing my finger deeper inside her. "I want more. Gimme your cock, baby!" she whisper-yelled.

I looked down at her, totally in shock. I fucking loved dirty-girl Race. "Say it again."

She spread her legs. "Fuck me, Morgan."

It wasn't the same, but it made my cock leap at her words.

"You don't have to tell me twice," I said as I pressed the tip of my cock against her wetness, removed my finger, and thrust inside.

"Jesus," she murmured as I leaned forward, pulling out and pushing back inside her with more force.

"You feel so damn good," I moaned against her neck, pounding into her.

"Yes. Yes," she chanted as I covered her mouth with my hand, quieting her.

The desk jumped, moving with each thrust as I pummeled her pussy, driving deeper with each stroke.

"Everything okay in—" James asked as he walked through the door and froze.

I looked up, burying myself inside her.

Race covered her face. "Oh God."

I smiled, feeling like I was officially a member of the team. I'd christened my office and been caught for the first time.

"Looks like you're doing okay," James said, laughing quietly. "I'll let you get back to *work,*" he teased, backing up and getting one last look before closing the door.

"Oh my God," Race said, her voice muffled by her hands.

"It's okay." I started to move inside her again.

"You're going to be in trouble," she whispered as she uncovered her face.

"No, I'm not," I said, driving my cock as deep as it would go.

"We can't..."

"Just wrap your legs around me and enjoy the ride, princess," I said through gritted teeth.

Gripping her tits, I held on to her chest, squeezing them in my hands as my dick plunged in and out of her wetness.

Her body thrashed, sliding against the desk as I shoved my cock inside her. I bit my lip, quieting the moans that threatened to escape as I battered her pussy over and over again.

She bore down, gripping the desk tighter as she fucked me back, slamming her core against me. As my balls slapped her ass, I felt the familiar tightness and tingle in my spine.

"I can't last," I warned, hoping she was close.

"Just a little more." She jammed herself down on my hard length.

"Fuck," I moaned, trying to hold out just a little longer.

"Yes. Right there." Her head tipped back and her body halted, gripped by the orgasm ripping through her system and squeezing the life out of my dick.

She sent me over the edge as my vision blurred and my breath hitched in my throat. I slowed my stroke, enjoying the feel of every inch sliding in and out as I came inside her.

I collapsed, hovering over her body with my shaky arm as I tried to catch my breath.

"I can't believe we just did that," she whispered, sucking in air like a fish out of water.

"It was fuckin' amazing." I pushed myself up as my cock began to soften inside her.

She sat up on her elbows, watching me as I pulled my pants up and tucked everything inside. "I could get used to a lunch break like this," she said with a lopsided, post-orgasm smile.

"Only if you're working with me, princess," I said, zipping my pants as I walked over to retrieve her panties.

She tipped her head, watching me upside down. "I can't work with you."

"Why not?" I thought it was an amazing idea. She needed a job; why the fuck not work here with me?

"I have a few ideas, and they don't include working here."

I opened my desk drawer, dropped her panties inside, and shut it with my knee.

"Hey," she yelled, sitting up and reaching for the drawer.

"Don't," I said, shaking my head at her and keeping my leg flush against the handle.

"I need those," she whined, trying to move my leg away but not succeeding.

"No panties, remember?" I cocked an eyebrow as I stared down at her, still spread-eagle and half naked on my desk.

"Fine. I have more where those came from." She slid off the desk. "I have to clean up," she said, looking around my office.

"Here." I grabbed a few tissues off the bureau and handed them to her.

"It would be easier if I had my panties back," she said, wiping herself and tossing the tissues in the trash. "Please."

I grabbed her around the waist, pulling her close and giving her a kiss. "Oh no you don't," I told her, brushing my nose against hers. "No panties when you're with me."

"Why?" She placed a hand on my neck and looking up at me.

"Cause I want to be able to taste you whenever I want."

She chewed her lip before she nodded.

"See how easy that is when you do what I want?" I asked as I pushed her skirt down, helping her fix it.

"You can be a bully." She smoothed the black material with her fingertips.

"But you like me that way," I teased, reaching out and holding her hand.

"Eh," she muttered.

"Race," I whispered then waited for her to reply.

"Yeah?"

"I love you," I said, feeling so much happiness that I thought I'd explode.

"I love you too, Morgan."

I was the luckiest son of a bitch in the world.

CHAPTER THIRTY-FOUR

RACE

New Beginnings

"Where are we going?" he asked, shifting in his seat.

He still wasn't comfortable with me driving Elvira. I loved messing with his head when I drove. He was too easy.

Every time he'd flinch or grab the dashboard, I'd giggle. It didn't have much to do with his darling car, but more about giving control up to me.

"I want to show you something." I glanced at him out of the corner of my eye.

"It's barren around here," he said as he looked out the window.

"There's so much open space around here. That's why it's perfect."

"What is?" He turned his attention toward me.

"My surprise."

"I hate surprises," he grumbled.

"Just sit there and enjoy the ride." I pressed down on the gas pedal and Elvira took off like a bat out of hell.

"Race," he said, reaching out to grab the dashboard.

"Are you worried I'm going to hit a cow?" I teased, gripping the steering wheel tighter as I stared straight ahead. "Look around, Morgan. There isn't a thing for miles but trees, sunshine, and open road."

"Are we almost there, at least?"

I enjoyed every moment of anxiety I was causing him. "Yes."

"Did you buy a farm?" He dragged his hand across his face.

"No. Just relax, baby. We're only two miles away," I told him, looking for the hidden drive.

"Thank God," he said, pulling his collar out and fanning himself.

As I turned down the dirt road lined with pine trees, the sign finally came in to view.

He turned toward me. "You're bringing me to the driving course?"

I nodded, bouncing in my seat. "It's not just any course," I told him, unable to wipe the smile off my face as I glanced at him. "It's the place where I spent my childhood with my father. This is Johnny's place."

"You're going to make me sit in a car and speed around a dirt course?" His face paled. "Are you trying to kill me?"

"You can drive your own car." I pulled into the empty parking lot.

"I can't ruin Elvira."

I rolled my eyes. "You can drive one of the other cars. I wanted you to see this place."

"It's important to you, huh?" He relaxed as I parked the car.

"Very." I turned the car off and sagged into the seat.

I looked around, taking in the place that held so many happy memories for me as a child. It hadn't changed a bit. It was still an out-of-the-way, hidden course for those who followed the circuit. It was where many drivers got their feet wet before heading out to join the big leagues.

"I have something to tell you. I've been waiting until now to share the news," I whispered.

His eyes grew wide as his lips parted. "Are you…" His voice trailed off as he swallowed. "Pregnant?"

I covered my eyes, shaking my head. "God, no."

"Phew," he muttered, wiping his forehead. "I mean, maybe someday, but we haven't been a couple that long."

I raised an eyebrow as a grin danced on my lips. "I didn't know we were officially a couple," I said, totally yanking his chain.

"I told you you're mine, Race."

I clasped my hands together and hunched my shoulders. "You're always so romantic."

He threw his hands up as he exhaled. "Do you want me to get down on one knee?"

It was my turn to have the blood drain from my face. "No, Morgan. I mean, I love you, but you could ask me to be your girlfriend."

"Race, do you wanna go steady?" He smirked.

"You're such an asshole sometimes." I laughed, shaking my head.

His mouth dropped open as he held his hands out. "What did I do?"

"I want to be romanced, bonehead. A little more effort than what you just did."

He clucked his tongue against the roof of his mouth and rubbed his chin. "I'll come up with a plan."

I covered my mouth. "Now that's romantic," I mumbled into my palm.

"So, what's the news?"

"I decided what I want to do with the rest of my life," I told him, glancing at the building in front of us. "I bought the track from Johnny. I'm the proud new owner."

His mouth fell open as he stared at me.

"I'm going to make this the best damn course in central Florida." I waited for his response.

"I'm speechless," he said as he looked at the building and back to me. "You bought it already?"

I nodded, unable to stop smiling. "We're here to sign the papers."

"No more corporate world?" he asked, tilting his head.

"No. I figure I can use my background to bring this baby back to life. I'll bring Cara to help me, and we'll have this sucker hopping in no time."

A slow, lazy smile spread across his face as he leaned over and took my hand. "I'm excited for you. You're finally following your dreams."

I sighed, squeezing his hand as I stared into his eyes. "For the first time in a long time, I feel like I can breathe again. I've never been so excited about anything in my life, Morgan."

He motioned toward the track. "Want to show me around your place?"

"Yes." I released his hand.

We strolled toward the offices hand in hand, and I resisted the urge to skip. I felt like a kid again as we walked the halls that hadn't changed in twenty years.

"You have a lot of work to do." Morgan glanced around.

I squeezed his hand, peering up at him. "I know, baby. I can do it," I told him.

"I know you can. You can do anything you put your mind to. You're the most amazing woman I've ever met."

My cheeks now ached from the happiness I could no longer contain.

"Ms. True," said a man as he waited in the hallway outside the conference room. "We've been waiting for you."

"Here goes nothing," I said to Morgan, taking one last breath before walking inside and changing my future forever.

"You did it, kid," Johnny said as he wrapped his arm around my shoulder and pulled me against him. "Your dad would be so proud of you."

I glanced up at him, feeling the bittersweet sorrow in that truth. "I know, Johnny. I wish he'd been here to see it."

"He's watching over you, Race."

I swallowed hard. "I hope so." I blinked the tears away.

"What's the first order of business?" he asked as we gazed out over the track from the grandstands.

I looked over at Morgan as he surveyed the place. "I want to take him out on the track. He needs to experience what I feel when I'm out there."

"I don't want to go out there," Morgan interrupted as he walked toward us.

"Oh, yes you do." I glanced at Johnny and winking. "Trust me."

He grumbled, rubbing the back of his neck as he watched a car speed around the bend. "As long as I get to drive."

Johnny kissed the top of my head. "I'm going to let you two kids have some fun. I'm going to clear out my office."

I reached out, touching Johnny's arm. "I wanted to talk to you about that," I said, hoping he'd say yes.

"I'm all ears."

"I want you to stay on here and work with me," I told him, stroking his arm.

"I'd love to, kid. I want to spend more time at home, but I'll be here to help with anything you need."

"Johnny, you're the last link I have to my dad. This course has been yours since before I was born. It wouldn't be right not to have you here. You have a place here, with me, for as long as you want."

"You've made me the happiest man in the world, Race," he said and hugged me tightly.

Resting my head on his chest, I imagined that my father was hugging me, like he had so many times in this place. The familiar sounds and smells brought me back to my childhood.

"Thanks, Johnny," I mumbled into his chest, trying to hold on to the memory of my father.

"You two be careful out there, you hear?" He released me, glancing between Morgan and me.

"We will be, sir," Morgan replied.

"Are you ready to have some fun?" I asked Morgan, shaking with excitement.

Morgan didn't look so sure as he glanced back at the track.

"Should I call an EMT to be on standby in case he," Johnny said in my ear, motioning at Morgan, "has a heart attack out there?" He laughed quietly, causing me to giggle.

"He'll be fine," I told him, looking over at Morgan. "Once I get him out there, he'll relax."

"What are you two whispering about?" Morgan asked, walking toward us.

"Nothing."

"Liar," he growled, wrapping his arms around my waist.

I pulled our bodies toward the stairs, unable to wait another minute to get behind the wheel. "Come on, sissy. Let's get on that track."

He brushed his lips against my forehead. "Show me what makes you tick, princess."

"Hold on to your pants, big boy. I'm about to blow your mind," I teased him, patting his belly as we walked down the steps.

"I'd rather you blow something else." He glanced down at his crotch.

"If you're a good boy, maybe I'll reward you," I teased as I let my hand slide down his back and squeezed his ass.

He peered down at me, blocking the sun from my eyes with his size. "Baby, I eat your pussy every day and you're still a pain in the ass."

"I allow you the pleasure of tasting me because I love you. Feel lucky, big boy," I teased him as we set foot on the track next to the waiting car.

"I'm the luckiest son of a bitch in the world," he muttered as he stopped next to me, looking over the sleek, sexy red car in front of us.

I patted his stomach. "You are."

"I'm driving, right?" he asked, running his hand along the hood.

"You are," I said, letting him go to walk around the vehicle. "I'll be with you. I'm going to teach you everything you need to know."

"How fast does she go?" he asked, glancing at me from the other side.

"How fast do you want to go?" I cocked an eyebrow.

"I feel the need. The need for speed."

"All right, Maverick. Climb in and buckle up," I told him. "Let's see how big your balls are."

"Princess, I know you have a set, but let's not forget whose are bigger."

"You'll have to remind me later." I smiled at him as we climbed inside and buckled ourselves in.

"You shared your fantasy with me, making it real. Tonight, I'm going to show you mine." He smirked, biting the corner of his lip.

My belly flipped from the burning in his sapphire eyes. "I don't know if I like the sound of that."

"Don't worry." He laughed. "I'm going to make you mine tonight. In every single way possible."

I laughed, laying my head against the seat. "Going to ask me to go steady again?"

"You're going to have to wait to find out. Today is a day for new beginnings and celebrations."

"Ready?" I took a deep breath.

"More than ever." He gripped the steering wheel, feeling the leather under his fingertips.

Morgan understood the happiness I felt on the track as he took the corners like a pro.

Driving around the track, leaving everything else behind, we both felt the freedom it offered.

As he drove, I took a moment to take stock of my life. So much had changed in a short amount of time. I hadn't imagined I'd quit my job and be a business owner.

On top of that, I'd never in a million years thought I'd be head-over-heels in love with the man who'd saved my life. Not just from Natasha, but also from the mundane existence I'd accepted as my reality.

CHAPTER THIRTY-FIVE

MORGAN

Mine

I'd fantasized about Race all day as we sped around the track, feeling everything else drift away. It was the best fucking day ever, but it was about to get even better.

"What's your fantasy?" She peered up at me with uncertainty in her eyes.

I undressed her slowly, taking time to appreciate all of her beautiful curves and delicious scents. I pressed her front against the wall, pulling her top over her head, breathing in the smell of her vanilla-scented hair.

"You'll see." I leaned forward and nibbled her neck.

I found the clasp to her bra and released it, letting it drop it to the floor. As I pressed my hardening cock against her, I unbuttoned and pushed her pants down.

"Not even a hint?"

"It's a surprise," I said, repeating the phrase she'd used earlier today.

"I hate surprises." She shuddered as I slowly kissed my way down her shoulders to the small of her back.

I reached up, pressing her chest against the wall and pulling her hips toward my mouth to give me better access. I slowly licked between her cheeks, to her asshole, and past it to her wet pussy.

She jumped, pressing her ass into my face. She pressed harder against my mouth as I pushed the tip of my tongue into her, penetrating her ass. I moved my hand to her entrance and inserted a finger after a few up and down strokes, and I moved two fingers inside her. Her ass was slick with saliva as I nudged a finger against the tightness.

She jumped again, yelping softly. "What are you doing?"

"Shh, baby. It won't hurt. It's only a finger. Relax."

A moment later, as I fingered her pussy, she relaxed and pressed back, allowing my finger to enter her asshole. Slowly, I moved them in rhythm, with one finger in her ass and two in her pussy, all while nibbling on her ass cheeks.

She started to gyrate her hips in unison with my hand as I gently pressed a second finger into her ass. She paused, adjusting to the added digit before she started to move back and forth with increased speed.

Just as I felt her approaching orgasm, I removed my fingers.

She peered over her shoulder, glaring at me. "I was about to come."

"Not like this, princess. I need to be inside you," I said with a grin on my face as I stood. "Lie on the bed."

She walked to the bed as I made my way to my dresser. I opened the drawer and removed the restraints. I needed her to keep still for what I had planned for her. I'd claimed most of her body, along with her soul, but I needed to know she was mine and always would be.

"What do you think you are going to do with those?" she asked with wide eyes.

I sat down, brushing my hands against her cheek. "Do you trust me, love?"

"Yes."

"Do you believe I won't hurt you?" I swallowed hard, silently praying that she'd say yes.

"Yes," she said.

"I want to tie you up so you can't squirm away from the mind-bending orgasm I am about to give to you," I said, knowing that once I had her tied down, her ass was mine for the taking. "Is that okay with you?"

She nodded, lying back. "Yes."

"Never. I'll never hurt you," I promised, moving to the right side of the bed. Holding one strap in my hand, I tossed the others on the bed.

"I know you wouldn't."

I leaned over, whispering in her ear as I placed her hand in the loop. "I promise to bring you more pleasure than you've ever had in your life. Have you ever been tied up or restrained sexually before?" I asked as I tightened the rope around both of her wrists.

"No. Never trusted a man enough to let him. I won't lie, though—I used to fantasize about it." Her cheeks turned pink as she bit her lip.

"I'll be gentle, and I won't hurt you." I attached the rope to the headboard, both hands together over her head, and moved toward her foot before taking it in my hand.

She pulled her foot from my grasp, holding it in the air. "You're not going to leave me here tied up or some shit, are you? 'Cause I swear to God, I'll kill you in your sleep."

Tough-girl Race was sexy as fuck. "I just don't want you wiggling your sweet ass away from me."

After I'd restrained her, I stood at the foot of the bed, staring down at her. There she was, spread-eagle and all mine to do with as I wished.

I took one of my pillows and slid it under her ass, elevating her for easier access. I dropped my jeans to the floor and crawled onto the bed, positioning my dick in front of her face.

"Open." I pressed the tip to her lips.

She obliged, opening wide and taking every inch as her eyes stared into mine.

I liked her like this, totally at my mercy. Maybe it was her strong personality, her need to be in control, or her smart mouth, but having her completely under my control gave me a euphoric feeling that I couldn't get enough of, and I prayed that it would never go away.

As her tongue stroked my cock, I turned, touching her nipple. It instantly hardened under my touch. Moving my hand down her belly, I brushed my fingertips along her skin until I reached her slickness. Just as she was starting to grind her mound against my hand, I pulled my hand back and landed a gentle smack to her pussy.

"Argh," she muttered with wide eyes, my cock filling her mouth, muffling her words.

"Never had your pussy spanked before?"

She shook her head, opening her mouth and letting my dick fall from her lips.

"No?" I lightly smacked it again.

She yelped, her body rising from the bed.

"You liked that, didn't you?" I asked, watching her body flush.

"Yes," she mumbled, relaxing back into the bed.

I crawled down her body and settled between her legs, taking in her beauty. I increased my pace and the pressure of each tap as her body arched up, meeting my hand with every smack.

"Yes." She panted.

I needed to feel her from the inside again. Pressing two fingers into her wet pussy, I slowly moved them in and out. She was close, closer than she was before, as I felt her pussy clench around my fingers.

Leaning forward, I sucked her clit into my mouth, stroking it with my tongue. She pulled at the restraints, trying to get closer. Damn, she tasted so fucking good. I could've eaten her pussy all day, but that wasn't part of my plan.

I wanted the one thing no man had ever had from her before. Nothing, not even the sweetness of her on my tongue, would cause me to lose focus.

As her body started to shudder and her head tossed from side to side, I quickened my pace.

Her hips arched off the pillow as her pants grew louder and her insides began to contract. "Yes! Yes! Yes! Morgan, fuck me with your fingers."

Removing my mouth, I spanked her pussy and fingered her as she came. "That's it, baby. Come for me. Feel me deep inside you," I murmured, forcing my fingers deeper as I pushed on her G-spot.

Liquid gushed from her pussy as she writhed. "Oh my God!" she wailed as her breathing faltered. She gasped for air. "What the hell was that?" she asked as she tried to pull a breath in.

I kept my fingers inside until her muscles stilled. "You squirted," I replied, completely shocked. I'd never in my life experienced something so...so spectacular. It was a complete turn-on.

I'd heard of women squirting, but I had never experienced it firsthand.

"Oh. My. God. I have never done that before," she mumbled, closing her eyes.

My cock was about to break off as I sat there, letting her catch her breath and come down from her high. Leaning forward, I drew her wetness into my mouth.

"Delicious."

If I didn't come, I was afraid my balls would be permanently blue. I moved between her legs, rubbing the head of my cock on her entrance, and then pushed it in to the hilt. She was so fucking wet that I almost lost it.

I stilled before I pulled back and slammed myself deeper. I thrust into her, each stroke a little harder as she arched her back to accommodate my length.

"Jesus, you're so tight," I whispered. Her pussy hadn't relaxed yet, still tense from the orgasm that had gripped her body moments ago.

"Fuck me, Morgan. Fuck me hard." Her body met my thrusts. "I love how your cock fills me," she murmured before I kissed her lips, silencing her.

Doing as she'd asked, I crashed into her—over and over until she came again. But even though my plan was to take her in the one way she hadn't been taken, I couldn't resist. The feel of her pussy milking my cock drove me over the edge and had me grunting through the pleasure that racked my body.

My legs trembled, every hair on my body stood up at attention, and my breathing stopped completely. As I spilled into her, my vision blurred and tiny sparks burst behind my closed eyes. I tried to hold myself up, not wanting to crush her under my weight. As my arms shook from the pressure, I rode the last wave of the orgasm that I hadn't been able to stop from happening.

"Fuck." I rolled to her side, trying to get air in my lungs.

"What's wrong?" she asked, her panting matching mine.

"That's not how I wanted that to go," I said, wiping the sweat from my brow.

Her body shook as she giggled. "I think it turned out pretty well for both of us."

"Says the woman who squirted all over the bed." I sat up and untied her feet.

"Sometimes we get what we need and not what we plan. You taught me that, Morgan."

"Oh, I need that." I reached over and stroked the side of her ass. "Turn over," I commanded, giving her thigh a quick slap.

"I don't think I could come again," she whined. "Plus, I still have this," she said as she wiggled her arms in the restraints above her head.

I unfastened her ankles, rubbing the red marks left behind by the ropes. "That's not a problem." I flipped her onto her belly.

"Well, fuck," she blurted, pulling on the single restraint that held her hands. "But I—"

"You will. I'm going to give you so many orgasms that you'll never want to leave me."

"I'll die if you give me another," she mumbled into the pillow, burying her face in the material.

"Baby, it's the only way to go." I ran my hands along her ass cheeks.

She looked at me over her shoulder. "Morgan?"

"Yeah, princess?"

"I'm never leaving you, orgasms or not. You don't have to do this," she whispered as she glanced at her ass.

I squeezed the cheeks in my hands, feeling their softness. "But I do. I won't feel like you're mine unless I have every inch of your body."

"Just this once," she said. "I don't know if I'll like it."

"I'm going to give you an orgasm so intense I'm going to have to perform CPR on you when I'm done." I was going to do everything in my power to make her heart stop from bliss.

"I'm yours. Take me."

I stroked my shaft, making myself hard again as I kissed the silky skin of her back. I took her gentler than I ever had before, letting her adjust to the intrusion and get used to the feeling of my hardness in her ass. It didn't take long before her tiny moans grew, turning into screams of pleasure.

I'd like to say that I lasted long, bringing her over the brink time and time again. But taking Race in this way, claiming all of her, had me spiraling out of control and getting lost sooner than I wanted.

"Mine," I murmured against her back as I came.

I realized that the only thing that mattered to me was her. Having her with me each night, spending my days with her, and making love to her made my life feel complete.

Race had softened me as much as I had her. She made me want to be a better version of myself. No longer needing to protect the soldiers of my past, I made her safety and happiness my priorities.

I loved her.

She completed me.

I fuckin' hated that line from the cheeseball movie she'd made me watch last night, but in that moment I understood it.

In all honesty, I hadn't saved Race True. She'd saved me. Giving me a life full of love and everything I'd always needed but never knew I'd wanted.

I was nothing without her.

EPILOGUE

RACE

Today, I said the words, "I do."

Calm cascaded over me as I uttered the words, a peace I'd never known in my entire life.

I hadn't imagined they would be so easy to say, but they slipped from my lips like I'd always been meant to say them.

Morgan DeLuca was mine as much as I was his. He wasn't a selfish man, not the prick I'd thought he was when I met him a year ago.

At first, I'd wanted him for his looks, but when I'd really gotten to know the man and understood what made him tick, I hadn't been able to resist the pull he had over me.

How could I say no to a man who had rescued me twice? I loved him more than anyone, and I would be forever in his debt for everything he'd done to make me whole again.

His kindness and patience helped me get through the darkest days, and he still walks the journey with me now when I wake up screaming in the middle of the night.

"We did it," he said as we entered the church bridal room hand in hand.

"We did." I looked at my husband and smiled.

My husband.

It sounded foreign and perfect at the same time.

"Mrs. DeLuca." He drew me against his body.

"Husband," I murmured against his lips.

"Look at them. Think they'll make me a grandbaby tonight?" Fran asked as she walked into the tiny bridal room, interrupting our kiss.

I could feel the pink creep across my face as she spoke with Mrs. Gallo.

"If you're lucky, Franny. If you're lucky," Maria told Fran.

Morgan released my lips, turning us to face them. "Ma, seriously. What's the rush?" he asked as he shook his head, pulling me tighter against his side.

"I'm not getting any younger," Fran complained as she tapped her foot. "Just one."

"One too many," Morgan said, glancing down at me. "You want a baby right now, princess?" he asked, begging me to say no.

"Whatever Fran wants." I gave him a gigantic smile.

"Suck-up," he whispered in my ear.

"That's my girl." Fran came toward me. "Call me Ma."

"Ma," I whispered as my insides warmed.

"Just give her what she wants," Mike said as he entered the room. "Ma never shut up about it until Joe and Suzy got pregnant. Trust me," he added as he placed his arm on Morgan's shoulder. "Takes so much heat off you. It's amazing. Totally worth it."

"Says the man who won't change a diaper."

"I'm not crazy, woman," Mike replied, giving me a wink.

"Let's leave the kids alone so they can start on the baby as soon as possible," Fran said to everyone, trying to corral them out of the room.

"Ma, it's a church, for Christ's sake."

"Coming from your heathen ass, that's rich, Morgan."

"Mrs. DeLuca, let me escort you out and let the kids have a few moments," Johnny said as he grabbed Fran's hand and looped it into the crook of his arm.

Fran stared up at Johnny. "Anywhere you want to go, handsome."

Johnny took Fran out the door. He winked at me before leaving us alone.

"Don't egg her on, Race," Morgan pleaded with me, putting both arms around my back and smashing me against his chest.

"It's nice to have a mother, Morgan. You should be a little nicer to her sometimes."

"Babe, I'm as sweet as I can be with her. You give her an inch and she takes a mile."

"Did you see that?"

"What?" he asked, looking around the room.

"I think we have a new love connection."

He narrowed his eyes. "Who?"

"Your ma and Johnny."

"She needs someone in her life," Morgan said, surprising me at his coolness over the situation. "Maybe she'll forget about the babies."

"Speaking of babies." I cupped his cock in my hands. "Wanna practice?"

"Let's start right now. No time like the present, wife."

"It's a church, husband. We can't do that here."

He kissed me, nipping at my lip. "You're the one holding my balls. I think you already crossed the line.

We're already going to hell. Best to make sure we have a little fun along the way."

I chuckled, letting his mouth travel down my neck and settle near my collarbone. When I'd picked the dress out, it seemed like a good idea to have a high neckline to hide my scars, but as I stood here with his mouth traveling across my skin, I regretted my decision.

"I'll follow you anywhere," I whispered, tangling my hands in his hair.

"You'll be the death of me," he murmured against my skin.

"Till death do us part." I reached out and locked the door. "I'm yours forever."

"Mine," he grunted as he lifted me into his arms and carried me to the couch in the corner.

"We're definitely going to hell," I murmured as he lifted the hem of my dress before undoing the zipper on his tux pants.

"As long as we'll be together."

My husband. My love.

My savior. My family.

My everything.

The end is only our beginning

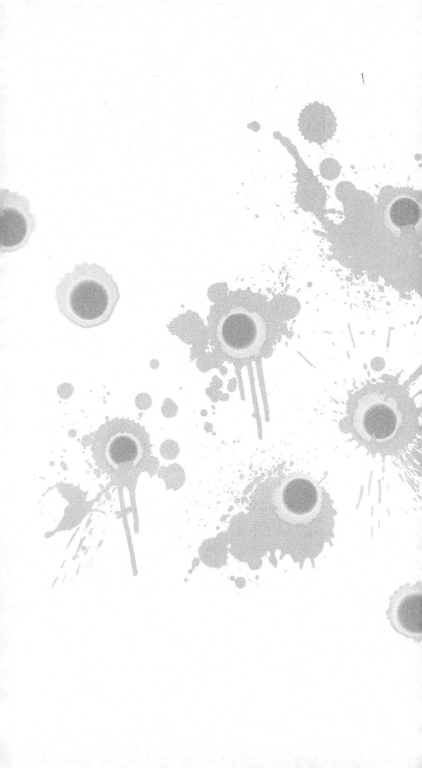

OTHER BOOKS BY CHELLE BLISS

To learn more about Chelle's book visit chellebliss.com

ABOUT THE AUTHOR

Chelle Bliss is the **USA Today** bestselling author of the **Men of Inked** and **ALFA Investigations** series. She hails from the Midwest, but currently lives near the beach even though she hates sand. She's a full-time writer, time-waster extraordinaire, social media addict, coffee fiend, and ex high school history teacher. She loves spending time with her two cats, alpha boyfriend, and chatting with readers.

JOIN THE MY NEWSLETTER
chellebliss.com/newsletter

www.chellebliss.com

FOLLOW ME
facebook.com/authorchellebliss1
twitter.com/chellebliss1
instagram.com/authorchellebliss

ACKNOWLEDGEMENTS

There are so many people that help in the creation of every book I write. I don't even know where to start, but here goes...

Cat Mason, thanks for lusting after my fictional men. I love that you're always willing to read my babies as soon as I offer it to you. Your support, love, and friendship have meant so much to me.

Tracy McKay...what can I say? I love you a ton. Although I've only wrapped my arms around you once, you'll always hold a special place in my heart. The messages you send me are priceless.

I can't thank the bloggers enough that have supported me over the last year and a half. You've been amazing. Thank you for loving the Men of Inked and your excitement for the new series. I hope you enjoyed meeting Morgan and Race. I know blogging is a tough job, but you do it with grace and kindness that I'll never forget.

I seriously think I have the best readers in the world. The messages and e-mails I receive every day drive me forward and keep my fingers banging out words on the keyboard. The way you embraced the Gallos had me dumbfounded. I hope that *Sinful Intent* was everything you'd hoped for and that the sneak peek into *Unlawful Desire* has you wanting more. I can't wait to bring the Neon Cowboy guys back into the fold. Hold on to your seats, it's going to be one wild ride.

None of it would be possible without my guy. He put up with my bitchy attitude, complete meltdowns, and stuck by my side. He made sure I had food, love, and held me when I needed it. Each day is a new adventure and I can't wait to see what the future holds. Thank you for being you and being by my side.

Lisa A. Hollett, my editor and friend, you are a rock star. Even in the process of moving across the country you found the time to edit SI and put up with my bullshit. Each day you made me laugh and your words were supportive and kind. Thank you for being along for the entire SI ride. I can't wait to see what we can do in the future. Look out LA, Lisa's on the way. Get the wine ready.

I have to thank Arran at Editing720. I'm sure your comments will make me wince and leave me wondering how badly you hated reading SI, but that's why I love you editing my work. You're dead honest, unyielding, and always find a way to make me laugh. I know romance isn't your favorite read, but thank you for taking the time to read each word. I think you'll be proud when you see I decreased the moans just for you, but probably to the dismay of my readers.

Thanks to Darren Birks and Felicia Lenarczyk for the amazing cover photo. I think you captured the essence of Race and Morgan perfectly. I appreciate how quickly you shot the cover and your professionalism through the entire process.

I don't have enough words to the authors who have supported me. Not just helping spread the word about the Men of Inked and *Sinful Intent*, but also for your help and encouragement. We truly are a family. Without each other we are nothing, but together we're a force that keeps the traditional publishing world on their toes.

To my good friend, Meredith Wild, I don't have words for you. You're always there to lend an ear and tell me how it is. You never hold back and remind me what's truly important. I'm so proud of everything you've accomplished and can't wait to see where you go from here.

Two people that always make me laugh are Aly Martinez and Mo Mabie. You girls are whores and I love you for it. You're always quick with a sassy answer that verges on assholiness. Mo, your laugh alone brings a smile to my face. Aly, your attitude and wordiness makes me happy. I love you both. I can't wait to squeeze you again. Aly, I'll even let you hump my leg because I love you so much.

Thank you to Rosarita Reader for proofreading *Sinful Intent* and always being willing to review my newest release. It was great meeting you in Vegas last year. Bloggers like you make the journey a little more special.

Mickey Reed has been amazing. Thanks for being the final set of eyes on Morgan and Race. Thank you for being an amazing editor and friend over the last year. I appreciate all the time you spent with me.

Thanks for Fiona Wilson for being the final set of eyes on Sinful Intent. I love your badass Aussie self.

I need to thank my beta readers. I drove them insane writing *Sinful Intent*. I think I went through at least three drafts, if not more. They were honest and kept me striving for more. I couldn't have survived without Renita, Mandee, Malia, Patti, Maggie, Stefanie, Ashley, Wendy, Deb, Kathy, and Kaylee. You girls kick ass and I'll always love you for your honesty.

For anyone I may have forgotten, please forgive me. I appreciate every person along my journey and the countless friends I've made along the way.

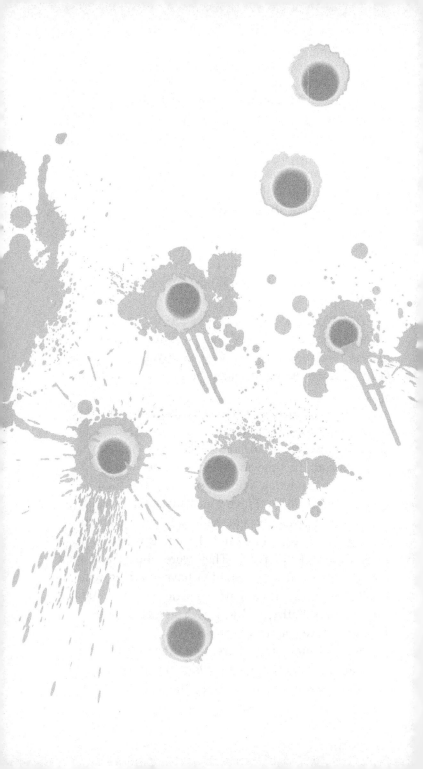

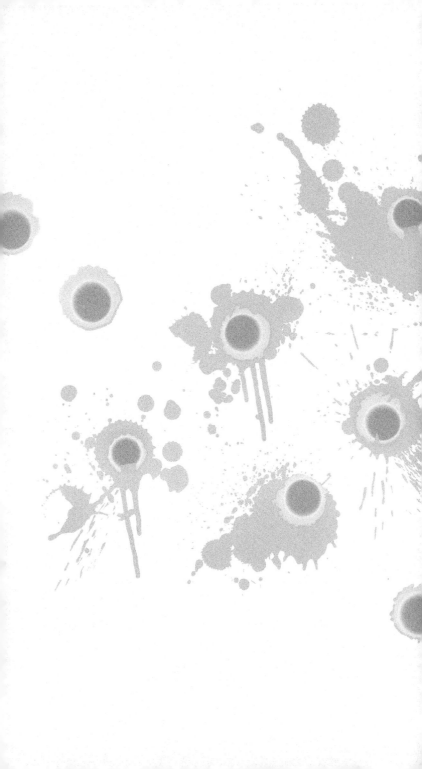

Made in the USA
Coppell, TX
14 June 2020